# Recipe Handbook for Live Aboard Caravanners

# &

# Motor Homers

## Cooking Whilst Living Aboard

*By Alastair McCloud*

# Forward

Having written two popular books called 'A Journey to a new life style books 1 and 2' that followed our life style whilst living aboard over the first few years of caravan life. We became passionate about collecting recipes from other likeminded campers. We had 'awning hopping' parties for birthdays and even Christmas and Easter holidays, and were always giving and receiving recipes. Whilst at Glen Coe in the Scottish Highlands we were given a recipe for Haggis (which I have not bored you with in this book) along with other weird and wonderful recipes. We began to gather together our vast collection of homemade food recipes which have brought back so many happy and wonderful memories, as we are now both in our seventies. We were fondly nicknamed Mr. & Mrs. Posh while working at the Camping & Caravanning Club Site Sandringham in Norfolk, when all the staff received an invitation to look around Sandringham House, ours being in the name of Mr. & Mrs. Posh, the credit of which for our nickname came from Mother Hen (the lovely camper and crafter Mrs. Cooper) and Miss Bridget who ran the camp shop next to the club site.  However, like everything you must plan, so do read the recipe book and choose what you would like to cook or not on your weekends away or your longer holidays. We have always carried a list of requirements for meals as you cannot carry 14 days' worth of food with you but with a list you can shop locally and cook up a storm of a meal in your mobile holiday home, as every tent, camper van, motor home, caravan is your space your holiday your escape from the daily routine. When we started out, I was desperately ill with asbestosis in both lungs with only a few years of expected life. I was the one who cooked all our meals while we were living in bricks & mortar, but when we took to the road it became great fun to share the cooking and we had moments of hysterical laughter when things went awry. Within one year of our life aboard my health did a turn round for the better, our happy carefree lifestyle had given us both a kick up the preverbal backside, and we began to take our health seriously and think what we were eating, for years we had poo pooed shopping at farm shops as an expensive gimmick, so a cheese toastie at lunch followed by a quick tea of something fried or out of a tin was ok, we were both overweight and soon got out of breath, me more so as I had COPD, no I was not a smoker but had lived in Birmingham during the 1960s and experienced the brown smog and with working for a manufacturer that made kilns for the bakery and pottery industries I inhaled asbestos which sat in my lungs until I reached my sixtieth year. But enough of my woes, the outdoor life and good simple cooking is our salvation, and now after fifteen years of being full timers we live in a beautiful cottage in Devon and thoroughly enjoy healthy cooking in our kitchen.

# Breakfast Index

1. Baked Eggs Brunch
2. Baked Salmon & Eggs
3. Banana & Honey Pancake Patties
4. Beans and Beans and More Beans
5. Berry Pancakes
6. Blueberry Omelette Roll Breakfast
7. Breakfast Pancake Wrap
8. Breakfast Potato Pancakes with Bacon & Eggs
9. Campers BBQ French Toast
10. Carrot Pancakes
11. Cook in the Bag Omelette
12. Cream Cheese & Mushrooms on Toast
13. Eggs with Marmite Soldiers
14. Four Way Pancake Wrap
15. Full English Potato Cake
16. Ham & Eggs Kedgeree Style Breakfast
17. Herb Omelette with Fried Eggs
18. Mushroom Hash with Poached Eggs
19. Quick Cooked Ham & Eggs Breakfast
20. Quinoa Porridge with Blackberries
21. Smoked Salmon with Poached Egg &Bacon
22. Spanish Eggs
23. Turkey Sausage & Eggs
24. Vegetable Breakfast Bake

Recipe 1

## Baked eggs brunch

**Prep**: 10 mins **Cook**: 30 mins
**Serves** 4
**Ingredients**

- 2 tbsp olive oil
- 2 leeks, thinly sliced
- 2 onions, thinly sliced
- 2 x 100g bags baby spinach leaves (torn)
- handful fresh wholemeal breadcrumbs
- 25g parmesan, (or vegetarian alternative), finely grated
- 4 sun dried tomatoes, chopped
- 4 medium eggs

**Method**

Heat the oven to 200C/180C fan/Gas mark 6. Heat the oil in a pan and add the leeks, onions and seasoning. Cook for 15-20 mins until soft and beginning to caramelise.

Meanwhile, put the spinach in a colander and pour over a kettle of boiling water. When cool enough to handle, squeeze out as much liquid as possible. Mix the breadcrumbs and cheese together.

Arrange the leek and onion mixture between 4 ovenproof dishes, then scatter with the spinach and pieces of sun-dried tomato.

Make a well in the middle of each dish and crack an egg in it. Season and sprinkle with cheese crumbs.

Put the dishes onto a baking tray and cook for 12-15 mins, until the whites are set, and yolks are cooked to your liking.

**Recipe 2**

## Baked salmon & eggs

Prep: 5 mins Cook: 10-15 mins
Serves 6

**Ingredients**

6 crusty white poppy seed rolls
25g butter, melted or use Garlic butter
6 slices smoked salmon
6 medium eggs

a few chives

**Method**

Heat oven to 180C/160C fan/gas 4.

Slice off the top of each roll, then gently remove the bread inside until there is a hole large enough to accommodate a slice of salmon and an egg.

 Arrange the rolls on a baking sheet, reserving the tops.

Brush the inside and edges of the rolls with a little melted butter, then arrange a slice of salmon inside each one.

Crack an egg into each and season.

Bake for 10-15 mins or until the eggs are cooked to your liking. Scatter with snipped chives.

Toast the tops, brush with the remaining butter, then cut into soldiers and use to dip into eggs.

**Recipe 3**

## Banana & Honey Pancakes patties

- Prep 10 mins Cook 15mins
- Serves 2
- 
- **Ingredients**
- 100g plain flour
- 2 large eggs
- 300ml milk
- ½ mashed banana
- Spoonful of clear honey
- Cinnamon to taste
- 1 tbsp olive oil, plus a little extra for frying
- 
- **Method**
- Put flour, eggs, milk, olive oil and a pinch of salt into a bowl or large jug, then whisk to a smooth batter.
- Set aside for 30 mins to rest if you have time or start cooking straight away.

- Set a medium frying pan or crêpe pan over a medium heat and carefully wipe it with some oiled kitchen paper.
- Pour pancake mix into the pan making 12cm round pancakes.
- When hot, cook your pancakes for 1 min on each side until golden, keeping them warm in a low oven as you go.

**Serve stacked**
On the base layer spread mashed banana Second layer, drizzle honey
Third layer, sprinkle on cinnamon lightly. Once cold, you can layer the pancakes between baking parchment, then wrap in cling film and freeze for up to 2 months.

**Recipe 4**

## Suggestions for Baked Beans for Breakfast, whatever else.

1. Baked beans on plain thick toasted bread
2. Baked beans on buttered toast
3. Baked beans on buttered toast with a poached egg
4. Baked beans on buttered toast with two hash browns
5. Baked beans on buttered toast with fried tomatoes
6. Baked beans on garlic butter toast
7. Baked beans on mayonnaise toast
8. Baked beans on peanut butter toast
9. Baked beans on beef spread buttered toast
10. Baked beans on buttered toast with melted grated cheese
11. Baked beans on buttered toast with chopped pork sausage

12. Baked beans on buttered toast with ham and fried egg
13. Baked beans on toast with fried gammon
14. Baked beans on toast with scrambled egg
15. Baked beans on toast with fried bacon squares
16. Baked Beans on toast with fried courgettes & red peppers
17. Baked beans on toast with fried black pudding
18. Baked beans on toast with a beef burger base
19. Baked beans on toast with cauliflower cheese on the side
20. Baked beans on toast with soft cheese base

**Recipe 5**

## Berry pancakes

Prep: 15 mins   Cook: 30 mins   Makes 10-12

**Ingredients**

50g self-raising flour
50g wholemeal or wholegrain flour
2 small eggs separated
150ml skimmed milk
berries and low-fat yogurt or fromage frais to serve

**Method**

Sift the flours into a bowl or wide jug, add the egg **yolks** only and a splash of milk then stir to a thick paste. Add the remaining milk a little at a time so you don't make lumps in the batter.

Whisk the egg **whites** until they stand up in stiff peaks, then fold them carefully into the batter – try not to squash out all the air.

Heat a non-stick pan over a medium heat and pour in enough batter to make a pancake about 10 cm across. Cook till both sides are light brown.

Keep warm while you make the remaining pancakes.

Serve with your favourite healthy topping.

Crushed Strawberries, Blackberries, Raspberries, Blueberries.

**Recipe 6**

## Blueberry omelette roll breakfast

Prep: 5 mins Cook: 2 mins
Serves 1

A one-egg omelette makes a high protein breakfast. If the brain-boosting berries aren't sweet enough, add 1 tsp honey

**Ingredients**

1 large egg
1 tbsp skimmed milk
3 pinches of cinnamon

½ tsp rapeseed oil
100g cottage cheese
175g chopped, blueberries, raspberries, or strawberries.

## Method

Beat egg with milk and cinnamon. Heat oil in a 20cm non-stick frying pan and pour in the egg mixture, swirling to evenly cover the base.
Cook for a few mins until set and golden underneath. There's no need to flip it over.
Place on a plate, spread over the cheese, then scatter with berries.
Roll up and serve.

**Recipe 7**

## Breakfast Pancake wrap

Eggs, bacon and a hash brown, all warmly hugged in a thin pancake wrap.
Servings 4 Wraps
Prep 30 mins
Cook 40 mins

## Ingredients

- **For the pancake wraps:**
- 2 large eggs

- A healthy pinch of salt
- 250ml skimmed milk
- 110g plain flour
- 1/2 teaspoon butter or try Garlic butter
- **For the wrap filling:**
- 4 hash browns
- 8 rashers streaky bacon (smoked or unsmoked)
- 4 tablespoons butter, divided
- two pinches of salt
- 4 large eggs
- 110g grated cheese

Brown or tomato sauce of your choice (optional)

**Method**

**Make the pancakes:**
In a medium-sized bowl, whisk eggs until lightly beaten. Add a pinch of salt and 1/3 of the milk and stir until combined. Add flour and whisk until smooth. While whisking, add the remaining milk. Batter should be thick and smooth.
Heat a 10-inch pan on medium-high and coat with butter. Drop approximately 2/3 of batter onto pan and cook until golden. You will start to see bubbles form on the top of the batter when it is close to being flipped. Flip over and repeat until golden. Keep pancakes warm on a plate until ready to assemble.
**Prepare the wrap ingredients:**
Preheat the oven to 220C/Gas mark 7. Line 2 oven trays with parchment paper.
Place 4 hash browns on parchment and bake until golden, approximately 20- 25 minutes. Place rashers of bacon on another sheet and bake until crispy, approximately 20 minutes.
While bacon and hash browns are baking, prepare the remaining ingredients for the wraps.
In a large non-stick pan, melt the remaining tablespoons of butter over medium heat. Crack the eggs into a medium-sized bowl with a pinch of salt and whisk until the eggs are just combined. Pour into the warm pan and turn heat down to medium-low. Cook eggs very slowly, swirling them in the pan using a wooden spoon or spatula (making scrambled egg). Eggs are done when they look silky, having come together and are still a little wet. Turn off the heat and add cheese. Mix to combine. Set aside.
**To assemble wraps:**
Spread the sauce of your choice in the middle of each pancake and place a hash brown on top. Place a quarter of the scrambled eggs on each hash brown. Layer bacon over the eggs.
Secure wraps in parchment until serving. They will keep up to a day in the fridge. Reheat in the oven or microwave before serving.

**Recipe 8**

## Breakfast Potato Pancakes with Bacon & Eggs

Prep: 15 mins Cook: 30 mins Serves 2 (makes 6 pancakes)

### Ingredients
- 140g floury potatoes, cut into large chunks
- 50g self-raising flour
- ½ tsp bicarbonate of soda
- 3 large eggs
- 5 tbsp milk
- 3 spring onions, finely chopped
- 2 tsp sunflower oil
- knob of butter
- 6 rashers of streaky bacon (smoked or unsmoked)
-

- **Method**
- Put the potatoes in a large pan of salted water and boil until tender. Drain well, tip back into the pan, shake for 1 min over a gentle heat to dry them off, then mash and leave to cool.
- Put the cooled mash in a bowl with the flour and bicarb. Whisk 1 egg with the milk, season, tip into the bowl and whisk until smooth. Stir in the spring onions, reserving some to serve.
- In a non-stick frying pan, heat half the oil and butter until sizzling, then spoon in half the pancake batter to make 3 pancakes. Cook for 1 min or so on each side until browned and set underneath, then flip and cook the other side. Keep warm in the oven while you make 3 more pancakes.
- Wipe out the pan, add the bacon and sizzle until almost crisp. Push to one side and crack in the 2 remaining eggs – with a splash more oil if needed. Fry to your liking, then serve with the pancakes and bacon, sprinkled with the remaining spring onions.

**Recipe 9**

## Campers BBQ French toast

Prep 10 mins

Cook 15 mins

Serves 6

**Ingredients**

6 eggs

6 slices bread (try seeded wholemeal brown)

6 rashers bacon (smoked or unsmoked)

Tomato sauce (optional)

**Method**

Heat the BBQ. Place a drizzle of oil on the BBQ hotplate.

Beat eggs (in a wide enough bowl to fit the bread).

Soak each slice of bread on both sides in the egg and place on BBQ hotplate, once cooked turn.

While the French toast is cooking, cook the bacon as desired on another BBQ hotplate.

Top French toast with bacon and serve with your choice of BBQ or tomato sauce.

**Recipe 10**
# Carrot pancake

Prep 10mins
Cook 10 mins
Serves 2

**Ingredients:**

125g wholemeal self-raising flour
50g grated carrot
2 eggs lightly beaten
220g milk
1 tbsp olive oil
Butter for frying pan
Cream cheese to serve

**Method:**

Combine all ingredients into a bowl and mix together to form a batter.
Heat up either the BBQ or a frying pan.
Add butter or spray lightly with oil.
Pour spoonfuls of mixture into frying pan or onto BBQ.
Flip when bubbles appear on one side and are lightly browned.
Remove pancakes when both sides are cooked
Serve hot with cream cheese (try Garlic soft cheese)

Recipe 11

## Cook in the bag Omelette

For the minimal camper
Prep 10 mins, Cook 15 mins
Serves 4

**Ingredients:**
- 8 eggs
- 100g tomato chopped
- 100g bacon, diced
- 50g grated cheese
- 2 shallots ends trimmed, thinly sliced
- 2 tbsp fresh parsley

- Salt and pepper
-

**Method:**

- Crack 2 eggs (per person) into a zip lock sandwich bag.
- Squeeze in palms of hands until eggs are mixed in the bottom of bag.
- Add finely chopped ingredients and parsley.
- Add salt and pepper and a tablespoon of grated cheese and squeeze until mixed well.
- Squeeze air out of bag and zip lock.
- Boil a pot of water on a flame or camp kitchen stove.
- Turn water down to a gentle bubble and place bags in (zip lock at top).
- Leave in water for 14 minutes.
- Once cooked, take out and roll onto plate = instant omelette,
- No washing up. Dispose of the bag respectfully

**Recipe 12**

## Cream cheese mushrooms on toast

Prep: 5 mins Cook: 5 mins
Serves 1

**Ingredients**

1 slice brown wholemeal seeded bread
1½ tbsp light cream cheese, plain or Garlic
1 tsp rapeseed oil
3 handfuls sliced small flat mushrooms
2 tbsp skimmed milk

¼ tsp wholegrain mustard
1 tbsp snipped chives
150ml orange juice freshly squeezed or from a carton

## Method

Toast the bread, then spread with a little of the cream cheese (don't use butter).
Meanwhile, heat the oil in a non-stick pan and cook the mushrooms, stirring frequently, until softened.
Spoon in the milk, remaining cheese and the mustard. Stir well until coated.
Tip onto the toast, top with chives and serve.
Pour a glass of your favourite juice.

**Recipe 13**

## Eggs with Marmite soldiers

Prep: 5 mins Cook: 5 mins
Serves 2

### Ingredients

2 eggs
4 slices wholemeal seeded bread
a knob of butter
Marmite
mixed seeds

### Method

Bring a pan of water to a simmer. Add 2 eggs, simmer for 2 mins then turn off heat. Cover the pan and leave for 2 mins more.

Meanwhile, toast 4 slices wholemeal seeded bread and spread thinly with butter, then Marmite. To serve, cut into soldiers and dip into the egg, then a few mixed seeds

### Recipe 14
### Four-way Pancake Wraps
Cook 10 mins

Prep10 mins

Serves 4 to 5 pancakes

**Ingredients**

!oo g of self-raising flour

2 eggs

200 ml of skimmed/full fat milk

**Method**

Sift the flour into a bowl. Make a well in the centre with the back of a spoon and break in the egg. Gradually whisk in the milk to make a thick batter, then add either the one of the pancake ingredients below, with some salt and ground black pepper.

Heat a little oil in a large frying pan. Using a large serving spoon, ladle the batter into the pan and cook one or two 12cm pancakes at a time, depending on the size of your pan.

When bubbles appear on the surface, carefully flip each pancake over. Cook for a few minutes more until golden brown underneath, then set aside.

**Recipe Tips**

**For lemon prawn pancakes**

Add 50g cooked peeled prawns (thawed, if frozen), 4 spring onions, (remove the darker green ends, chop the rest) and the juice of ½ lemon.

**Spicy chicken pancakes**

Add 85g cooked chicken, very finely chopped, 1 tbsp Balti curry paste, the juice of ½ lemon and 25g thawed frozen peas, chopped.

**For Tuna pancakes**

Add 50g Tuna tinned, 4 spring onions, (remove the darker green ends, chop the rest) and the juice of ½ lemon.

**Spicy Corned Beef pancakes**

Add 85g Corned Beef chopped, 1 tbsp Balti curry paste, the juice of ½ lemon and 25g thawed frozen peas, chopped.

Fold ingredient inside pancake

**Recipe 15**

# Full English potato cake

Prep: 20 mins Cook: 1 hr. 15 mins
Serves 6

**Ingredients**
1½ kg potato, peeled & diced into 1cm chunks
4 tbsp olive oil, plus extra for drizzling
spring onions, finely chopped
2 thyme sprigs, leaves stripped, plus 1 sprig left whole
25g butter melted, plus extra for greasing
12 rashers streaky bacon (cut the rind off)
3 large plum tomatoes, halved
cracked black pepper
6 medium eggs
buttered toast, to serve
brown/tomato sauce (optional)

**Method**
Bring a big saucepan of salted water to the boil. Put in the potatoes and simmer until almost tender, about 20 mins. Drain well and steam dry by returning the pan to the hob for a few mins. Then toss with 2 tbsp of the oil, spring onions, thyme leaves and a good amount of seasoning.

Grease your largest baking tray with some melted butter and press the potatoes into it. Put a baking sheet on top and gently press down to crush the potatoes into a cake. Cover and chill until ready for breakfast.

Heat oven to 220C/200C fan/gas mark 7. Drizzle the melted butter and remaining oil over the potato cake and bake for 30 mins until golden.

Place the bacon on the potatoes and bake for another 15 mins. Then dot over the tomato halves and the remaining thyme leaves, sprinkle with plenty of pepper, then crack the eggs among the gaps and bake for 5-8 mins, depending how you like your eggs.

To serve, cut the potato cake into 6 portions, along with the eggs, bacon, and tomatoes. Serve with the buttered toast, and brown and tomato sauce, (if required).

**Recipe 16**

## Bacon and Eggs kedgeree style Breakfast

Prep: 5 mins. Cook: 15mins.
Serves 4

### Ingredients

4 eggs
500g microwave long grain rice
1tbsp olive oil
1 onion, finely chopped
180g smoked bacon lardons
¼tsp cayenne pepper
handful fresh parsley, roughly chopped

### Method

Bring a pan of water to the boil and cook the eggs for 6-8 minutes. Drain and cool in running cold water, then peel and quarter. Cook the rice following the pack instructions.

Meanwhile, heat the oil in a frying pan over a medium heat and cook the onion and lardons for 5 minutes, until they're just becoming golden. Stir in the cayenne pepper and cook for a minute.

Stir through the cooked rice and serve topped with the quartered eggs, lardons and fresh chopped parsley.

**Recipe 17**

## Herb omelette with fried Eggs

**Prep:** 5 mins
 **Cook:** 5 mins
Serves 2

### Ingredients

1 tsp rapeseed oil
3 tomatoes, halved
4 large eggs
1 tbsp chopped parsley
1 tbsp chopped basil

### Method

Heat the oil in a small non-stick frying pan, then cook the tomatoes cut-side down until starting to soften and colour. Meanwhile, beat the eggs with the herbs and plenty of freshly ground black pepper in a small bowl.

Scoop the tomatoes from the pan and put them on two serving plates. Pour the egg mixture into the pan covering the base forming your omelette cook until set, remove from heat

Cut into four and serve with the tomatoes.

**Recipe 18**

## Mushroom hash with poached eggs

Prep: 10 mins:
Cook: 17 mins
Serves 4

**Ingredients**

1½ tbsp rapeseed oil
2 large onions, halved and sliced
500g closed cup mushrooms, quartered
1 tbsp fresh thyme leaves, plus extra for sprinkling
500g fresh tomatoes, chopped
1 tsp smoked paprika
4 tsp omega seed mix   (buy at Tesco)
4 large eggs poached

**Method**

Heat the oil in a large non-stick frying pan and fry the onions for a few mins. Cover the pan and leave the onions to cook in their own steam for 5 mins more. Add the mushrooms with the thyme and cook, stirring frequently for 5 mins until softened. Add the tomatoes and paprika, cover the pan and cook for 5 mins until pulpy. Stir through the seed mix.
Poach all four eggs, divide the hash between four plates, sprinkle with thyme and black pepper and serve with the eggs on top.

**Recipe 19**

## Quick cooked ham & eggs breakfast

Serves 6

### Ingredient

12 eggs
100g ham or bacon, diced
2 tomatoes, sliced
75g grated cheddar cheese

### Method

Spray an oven tray with oil.
Place ham or bacon onto the bottom of tray.
Place a slice of tomato on top of ham/bacon.
Sprinkle cheese on top of tomato and add an egg on top.
Place tray onto BBQ and cook for 10-15 minutes, until eggs are cooked
Suggestion:
Cook bacon/ham slightly before adding to tray depending on taste

**Recipe 20**

## Quinoa porridge with blackberries

Prep: 10 mins.
Cook: 30 mins.
Serves 4.

- **Ingredients**
-
- 100g blackcurrant jam
- 50g redcurrant jelly
- Small handful fresh blackberries
- 1 tbsp pistachios, finely chopped
- **For the quinoa porridge**
- 125g quinoa
- 400ml milk
- 125ml water
- 2 tbsp brown sugar
- ½ tsp vanilla extract
- pinch of salt
-

**Method**

Place the quinoa in a saucepan and cook over a medium heat for 2-3 minutes until toasted, stirring frequently. Add the milk, water, brown sugar, vanilla extract and salt and bring to the boil, stirring well. Reduce to a simmer and cook for 25 minutes until thick and the grains are tender.

Meanwhile, combine the jam and the redcurrant jelly in a small saucepan, stir well to combine, then fold in the blackberries.

Spoon the quinoa porridge into serving bowls when ready and top with generous tablespoons of the jam mixture. Sprinkle the finely chopped pistachios on top and serve.

**Recipe 21**

## Smoked salmon with poached eggs & bubble & squeak

Prep: 5 mins. Cook: 15 mins. Serves 2

### Ingredients

1 tbsp rapeseed oil
140g white cabbage, finely chopped
2 spring onions, finely sliced
300g whole new potatoes
1 tbsp snipped chives
2 medium eggs at room temperature
75g cooked smoked salmon

### Method

Cook the potatoes in a pan of boiling water until tender, then drain.
Place the salmon in the bottom of the oven to warm through
Heat the oil in a non-stick frying pan. Sweat the cabbage and the spring onions in the pan for a couple of mins. Meanwhile, chop and crush the potatoes roughly, then add to the pan along with the chives. Cook for 4-5 mins, flip it over (don't worry if it breaks) and cook for a further 4-5 mins.
Meanwhile, bring a small pan of water to the boil, then reduce the heat so it's just simmering. Stir the hot water into a whirlpool then crack the eggs into the

pan and simmer for about 3 mins until the whites are cooked and the yolk is just beginning to set. Remove with a slotted spoon and drain on kitchen paper.

To serve, divide the bubble & squeak between 2 plates, place the smoked salmon and poached eggs on top and grind over a little black pepper to taste.

**Recipe 22**

**Spanish Eggs**

Prep 10 mins. Cook 20 mins. Serves 6

- **Ingredients**:
- 
- 6 eggs
- 1 onion sliced thinly
- 1 clove garlic crushed
- 2-3 tomatoes, diced
- 1 red pepper diced
- ½ green pepper diced
- ½ yellow pepper diced
- 3 rashers bacon diced, smoked or unsmoked (optional)
- 2 chorizo sausages, diced
- 

**Method:**

In a large lidded frying pan, fry the sausages and bacon until cooked, then set aside.

In the same pan, fry the onion and garlic until soft.

Add peppers and cook until soft.

Add tomatoes, simmer for a few minutes until soft and sauce develops.

Return sausages and bacon to mix.

Make a hole in the mix and add the eggs and cover.

Allow eggs to poach in the liquid with other ingredients.

When poaching is completed to desired level, spoon eggs, sauce and onion mix onto plate.

TIP: Volume of ingredients can be varied depending on number of people.

**Recipe 23**

## Turkey sausage and egg breakfast

Prep time 10 mins.  Total cook time 30 min. Serves 4

**Ingredients**

- 350g lean minced turkey
- 4 Eggs
- 35 g red onion
- 1 1/2 tsp fresh rosemary
- ¼ tsp ground black pepper
- 1/2 tsp dried sage
- ¼tsp sea salt
- A dash sea salt
- 2 tbsp rapeseed oil
- 

**Method**

- In a large bowl, combine by hand the mince turkey, egg, onion, rosemary, ¼ teaspoon of the black pepper, the sage, and ¼ teaspoon of the salt.
- Pat to form four 10cm diameter patties.
- Add 1 tablespoon of oil to a frying pan and heat over medium-high.
- Place the sausage mixture into the hot frying pan and cook until browned and well done, about 4 minutes per side.

- Transfer patties to a warm plate loosely covering with foil.
- Add remaining tablespoon of oil to the frying pan and heat over medium. Add the eggs and cook until cooked to your liking, about 4 minutes.
- Top each sausage patty with an egg, and sprinkle with the remaining salt and pepper.
- Serve with a simple Rocket or tomato salad, to round out the meal.

**Recipe 24**

## Vegetarian breakfast bake

Prep 5 mins.
Cook 30 mins.
Serves 4

**Ingredients**

4 large field mushrooms
8 tomatoes, halved
1 garlic clove, thinly sliced
2 tsp olive oil
200g bag spinach
4 eggs

**Method**

Heat oven to 200C/180C fan/gas 6. Put the mushrooms and tomatoes into 4 ovenproof dishes. Divide garlic between the dishes, drizzle over the oil and some seasoning, then bake for 10 mins.

Meanwhile, put the spinach into a large colander, then pour over a kettle of boiling water to wilt it. Squeeze out any excess water, then add the spinach to the dishes. Make a little gap between the vegetables and crack an egg into each dish.

Return to the oven and cook for a further 8-10 mins or until the egg is cooked to your liking.

## Lunch Index

1.Baked Mushroom & Blue Cheese Risotto

2.Baked Potato & Chilli

3. Cajun Fry Chicken

4. Cheese & Bacon Chips

5. Cheese & Garlic Sausage Pancake Roll

6. Chicken & Broccoli

7. Chicken Fool

8. Chicken Rice & Peas

9. Chilli Chicken Drumsticks with homemade Chips

10. Courgette & Feta Fritters

11. Courgette & Bacon Frittata

12. Egg & Bacon Pie

13. Finger Licking Seasoned Chicken Drumsticks

14. Fragrant Chicken

15. Ham & Cheese Quiche

16. Mackerel Fish Cakes (tinned)

17. Leftover Chicken Recipe

18. Mushroom & Ham Omelette

19. One Pot Salmon & Asparagus

20. Parmesan Flavoured Chicken

21. Potato Roti & Egg

22. Portobello Mushroom Burger

23. Salmon with Beetroot Feta Salsa

24. Tomato Salsa Accompaniment

25. Tuna Cakes on Crumpets
26. Vegetarian Fresh Saag Paneer
27. Vegetarian Wrap

**Recipe 1**

## Baked Mushroom & Blue Cheese Risotto

Prep 10 mins.
Cook 45-55 mins.
Serves 2

## Ingredients

- 1 tsp olive oil
- 1 red onion, peeled and chopped
- 200g mushrooms, sliced
- 100g brown rice, rinsed
- 300ml vegetable stock (fresh or made with ½ cube)
- juice of ½ lemon
- 30g blue cheese, crumbled
- salt and freshly ground black pepper
-

**Method**

Preheat the oven to 200C/180C fan/Gas Mark 6.
Heat the oil in an ovenproof casserole dish, add the onion and fry for 3 minutes.
Add the mushrooms and fry for a further 2 minutes.
Add the rice and stir through, then add the stock and bring to a gentle simmer.
Cover with a lid and put in the oven. Cook for 45–55 minutes (reduce this to 20 minutes if you are using white rice), checking if you need to add more water halfway through, until the rice is tender.
Stir through the lemon juice and blue cheese.
Season to taste before serving

**Recipe 2**

**Baked Potatoes with Chilli Camp fire recipe**

Prep 10 mins. Cook 1 hr. Serves 4

**Ingredients**
4 baking potatoes
1 onion
1 tsp garlic
500 g minced meat
1 tsp cumin
1 tsp coriander
1 tsp paprika
1 tsp oregano Chilli Powder
400g tinned tomatoes
400g tinned four bean mix
120 mls water
Salt & pepper
Cheese
Chopped vegetables (optional)

**Method**
 Prick required number of potatoes with fork, wrap in foil. Place them on the coals at the edge of the campfire.
 Allow to cook for approximately 1 hr or until tender.
 Meanwhile make the chilli. Cook onion, garlic, and 500g minced meat in Dutch oven or large skillet until brown.
 Add the cumin, coriander, paprika, and oregano, and the same amount of chilli powder or as much as you prefer. Stir through.

Add the tin of tomatoes, the tin of drained four bean mix, and about 120 mls of water, also any chopped vegetables you may have available such as red or green peppers.

Season with salt and pepper. Allow to simmer, stirring frequently and adding water as required until potatoes are cooked.

**Recipe 3**

## CAJUN FRIED CHICKEN

Prep 5 mins. Ready in 15 mins. Serves 1

### Ingredients

1 × 150g skinless chicken breast
1 tsp sunflower oil

**For the spice mix)**
5 tsp ground cumin
2 heaped tsp smoked paprika
2 heaped tsp hot paprika
2 tsp dried thyme
2 tsp dried oregano
½ tsp cayenne pepper
1 tsp salt

### Method

For the spice mix, mix together the spices and salt.
Cut the chicken into 4–5 strips. Sprinkle 2 teaspoons of the spice mix into a plastic bag pop the chicken in and shake until the chicken is coated.

Heat the oil in a shallow frying pan over a medium-high heat. When hot, put in the chicken and cook for 4-5 minutes on each side, until golden and cooked through. Serve with a salad or vegetables of your choice.

Note

The spice mix here is enough to make 6–8 portions, so make a batch and store the rest of the spices in an airtight container or jar. For next time.

**Recipe 4**

## Mr. Posh's Cheese and Bacon Chips

Ready in 30mins including prep time.
Serves 4

### Ingredients

8 slices of bacon of your choice
170 g of hard cheese (Cheddar is good)
1 bag of oven ready chips

### Method

Preheat the oven to 200c/Fan 180/Gas Mark 6. Place the chips on a flat oven tray and cook for 20/25 mins or until the chips are brown.
Cut the bacon into 5mm squares (½ inch)
Place bacon in the frying pan and fry to your choice
Grate the cheese
Spread the bacon over the chips then spread the grated cheese and return to the oven until the cheese has melted.
Divide the bacon & cheese chips into four and serve.
A good standby for awning hopping

**Recipe 5**

## Cheese and garlic sausage pancake roll

Prep 40 mins.
Cook 50 mins.
Serves 6

### Ingredients

6 pork or chipolata sausages.
175g Cheddar cheese
75g garlic butter
450g plain flour
½ pint of skimmed milk
2 eggs
Pinch of salt and pepper
1 tbsp vegetable oil, plus a little extra for frying
Paprika
Cocktail sticks optional

### Method
### The Pancake base
Put the flour, eggs, milk, 1 tbsp oil and a pinch of salt into a bowl or large jug, then whisk to a smooth batter. Set aside for 30 mins to rest
Set a medium frying pan over a medium heat and carefully wipe it with some oiled kitchen paper. When hot, cook your pancakes for 1 min on each side until golden, keeping them warm in a low oven as you go.
Fry or grill the sausages until golden brown. Then slice the sausages down the middle putting a thin slice of garlic butter in. (Use a fork to steady the sausage while cutting it open)
Take your oven tray and carefully wipe it with oiled kitchen paper.

Roll the chipolatas in the pancake and place on the baking tray

When all six are wrapped and placed onto the oven tray. Sprinkle the grated cheese over the rolled pancake and a dusting of paprika.

Place in the oven on 200C/Gas mark 6 for five minutes or until the cheese has melted.

Serve with a side salad.

**Recipe 6**

## Chicken & Broccoli

Prep 15 mins.
Cook 20 mins.
Serves 2

### Ingredients
2 × 150g skinless chicken breasts
2 shallots
1 bay leaf
200g head broccoli, cut into florets
1 tsp olive oil
1 garlic clove, peeled and finely sliced
1 small red chilli, deseeded and finely chopped
6 Chestnut mushrooms diced
2 tbsp light soy sauce

### Method
Place the chicken breasts in the base of a lidded saucepan, together with 1 of the shallots cut in half and the bay leaf. Pour on boiling water until generously covered and bring to a gentle simmer for 5 minutes. Turn off the heat, put the lid on and leave the chicken to cook for a further 5 minutes. Check the chicken is cooked through before removing from the pan. Leave to cool slightly before cutting into slices.

Boil the broccoli by submerging in boiling water and simmering for 6 minutes until tender. Drain and set aside.

Chop the remaining shallot into fine half rings. Heat the olive oil in a wide frying pan over a medium heat and lightly fry the shallot and mushrooms until golden and soft. Add the garlic and chilli and fry for a further 2 minutes.

Stir in the cooked chicken and broccoli. Finally, add the soy sauce and warm through before serving

**Recipe 7**

# Chicken Fool

Ready in 25 minutes including 10 mins prep
Serves 2

## Ingredients

2 tsp olive oil
3 large free-range eggs, beaten
3 spring onions trimmed and shredded
½ garlic clove, peeled and finely chopped
250g cooked chicken, diced
1 tbsp dry sherry
1 small handful of fresh coriander leaves, chopped
salt and freshly ground black pepper

## Method

Heat 1 teaspoon of olive oil in a wide saucepan or wok, add the eggs and scramble lightly, removing them from the pan while they are still a little runny and just before they are fully cooked. Transfer to a bowl, cover and set aside.

Heat the remaining oil, add the spring onions and garlic and gently fry for a minute, then add the chicken and fry for a further 2 minutes.

Add the sherry and coriander, season to taste with salt and pepper and stir in the reserved eggs.

Cook for a further minute before serving.

**Recipe 8**

**Chicken, Rice & Peas**

Prep 10 mins.  Ready in 30 mins. Serves 2

## Ingredients

30g basmati rice (dry weight)
50g frozen peas
1 tsp olive oil
1 × 150g skinless chicken breast, cut into strips
75ml skimmed milk
½ tbsp light soft cheese
10g Mature Cheddar, grated
salt and freshly ground black pepper

## Method

Boil the rice as per the packet instructions. Add the frozen peas 6 minutes before the end of the cooking time. Drain and set aside.

Heat the olive oil in a frying pan over a medium heat and fry the chicken for 6-8 minutes, until browned all over.

Add the milk, soft cheese and Cheddar to the frying pan. Bring to a gentle simmer and continue to cook gently for 5 minutes.

Finally, add the cooked rice and peas to the pan and heat through. Season with salt and pepper.

Serve immediately.

**Recipe 9**

## Chilli Chicken Drumsticks with homemade Chips

Prep 10 mins
Cook 25 mins
Serves 4

### Ingredients

6 tbsp light soy sauce
2 level tbsp sweet chilli sauce
12 skinless chicken drumsticks
800g floury potatoes peeled and cut into chips
Frylight one-cal cooking spray
Mixed leaf salad to serve

### Method

Mix the soy and sweet chilli sauces in a wide bowl and season, make ¾ deep slashes in each drumstick, add to the bowl toss to coat evenly, Cover with cling film and chill for 30 minutes or overnight it possible.
Preheat your oven to 200C/Gas mark 6. Boil the chips for 3 to 4 minutes then drain. Spread on a non-stick baking tray in a single layer, spray with the Frylight and season. Bake for 20/25 minutes or until golden.
Meanwhile, preheat your grill to medium high. Grill the chicken for 15 to 20 minutes turning occasionally until golden brown and cooked through (the juices will run clear when you pierce the thickest part next to the bone.

Serve 3 drumsticks per person with chips and side salad

**Recipe 10**

## Courgette & Feta Fritters

Prep 10 mins. Ready in 30 mins. Serves 2

- **Ingredients**
- 
- 2 courgettes trimmed
- 3 spring onions trimmed and finely chopped
- 100g light feta cheese, crumbled
- A little fresh parsley, chopped
- 1 tsp dried mint
- ½ tsp paprika
- salt and freshly ground black pepper
- 1 level tbsp plain flour
- 1 large egg, beaten
- 1 tbsp olive oil
- 

## Method

Coarsely grate the courgettes and lay out on kitchen paper to dry out. Leave for about 10 minutes, then pat the top of the courgettes to remove excess moisture.
Mix the spring onions, crumbled feta, parsley, mint and paprika in a bowl. Season with salt and pepper and stir in the flour. Pour in the beaten egg and mix well. Finally, mix in the grated courgette.

Heat the oil in a wide frying pan over a medium-high heat. When hot, add 1 tablespoon scoops of the mixture to the pan, flattening each scoop with the back of the spoon as you go.

The fritters need to be widely spaced so you may have to do this in 2 batches. Fry for about 2 minutes on each side until golden. Serve immediately.

**Recipe 11**

## Courgette and Bacon Omelette

Prep 10 mins.  Cook 35 mins. Serves 4

**Ingredients:**

6 bacon rashers, chopped
1 tin sweetcorn drained
5 eggs
1 garlic bulb, crushed
1 tbsp dried rosemary
60 ml milk
1 tbsp olive oil
1 brown onion, chopped
50 g tasty cheese, grated
2 large Courgettes sliced
Salt and pepper.

**Method:**

Heat oil in a large non-stick frying pan. Add garlic, onion, bacon and courgettes and sauté until golden.

Mix together eggs, milk, cheese, rosemary and salt and pepper. Pour over the courgette mixture.

Sprinkle over the sweetcorn and cook over a low heat for 5 minutes. Place under a hot grill for a further 3-5 minutes or until browned.

**Recipe 12**

## Egg & Bacon Pie

Prep 10 mins.  Cook 30 mins. Serves 2

### Ingredients:

4 eggs, beaten
100g shortcrust pastry mix
250 ml milk
2 rashers bacon (smoked or unsmoked)
25g grated cheese
2 tomatoes, sliced
½ red pepper finely diced
¼ tsp pepper

### Method

Preheat oven to 180C/ Gas mark 4
In a bowl, add well beaten eggs to milk and pastry mix.
Pour into a greased large pie dish.

Add the bacon and red pepper.

Top with sliced tomato and grated cheese.

Sprinkle with black pepper.

Cook in oven for 25/30 minutes or until filling is set.

**Recipe 13**

## Finger licking seasoned Chicken drumsticks

Prep 5 mins.
Cook 30 mins.
Serves 4

- **Ingredients**
-
- 8 chicken drumsticks. 2 per person depending on appetite
- 1 tbsp mixed herbs
- 1 tbsp paprika
- 1 tbsp of plain flour
- 1 tsp of salt
- Pepper to taste
-

**Method**

- Preheat the oven to 200C/180C Fan/Gas 6.
- Lightly spray the drumsticks with Olive Oil.
- Put the mixed herbs, paprika, plain flour and salt into a plastic bag
- and shake to mix the ingredients together.
- Put the drumsticks into the bag and shake coating each drumstick with the mixture.
- Place the coated drumsticks onto a baking tray, and cook for 20-30 minutes

- or until the skin is golden and the chicken is cooked through. (To check, pierce the drumstick at its thickest part, next to the bone), if the juices run clear the drumstick is cooked
- Serve with veggies, salad, chips or on their own. Great hot or cold.
- Note
- Allow the chicken to marinate while you preheat the oven, this seasoning mix also goes well with white fish

**Recipe 14**

## Fragrant Chicken

Prep 25 mins.
Cook 30 mins.
Serves 2

### Ingredients
1 tsp olive oil
1 small onion, peeled and finely chopped
½ tsp cumin seeds
½ tsp turmeric
300 ml chicken stock
½ lemon
2 × 150g skinless chicken breasts, diced
200g new potatoes, quartered
2 tsp butter
6 chestnut mushrooms diced
4 fresh basil leaves roughly chopped
salt and freshly ground black pepper

### Method
Heat the oil in a pan over a low heat, add the onion and chestnut mushrooms and sweat for 7–8 minutes. Add the cumin seeds and turmeric and fry for 1–2 minutes until aromatic.

Pour in the chicken stock and bring to a gentle simmer. Add the lemon zest then cut out the flesh of the lemon, roughly chop and add to the pan.

Add the chicken, potatoes. Bring back to simmering point and cook gently for 10 minutes until the potatoes are tender and the chicken is cooked through. Remove the chicken and potatoes from the pan and keep warm.

Increase the heat under the pan to high and stir in the butter, basil and salt and pepper. Bubble over a high heat for 2–4 minutes until the sauce is a little thicker and glossy. Pour the sauce over the chicken and potatoes and serve immediately

Recipe 15

## Ham and Cheese Quiche

Prep 15 mins.
Cook 35 mins.

- **Ingredient**
- 
- Shop bought pastry to fit a deep 10" pie dish
- 1 tbsp butter or margarine
- 120g cooked ham, diced (off the bone)
- 1/2 teaspoon salt
- 350ml semi skimmed milk
- 30g plain flour
- 3 free range chicken eggs
- 1 tbsp Original Tabasco brand Pepper Sauce
- 120g Cheddar cheese, grated

### Method

Preheat oven to 180°C/Gas mark 4. Line a 10-inch deep pie dish with pastry. Cover the pastry with foil and weigh down with dried beans. Bake for 10 minutes. Remove beans and foil and bake 10 minutes longer or until crust begins to brown lightly. Cool.

Melt the butter in a pan over a medium heat. Add ham, onion, and salt. Cook for about 5 mins until liquid evaporates stirring occasionally. Remove from heat. Combine milk, flour, eggs, and Tabasco sauce in a medium bowl and beat until well blended. Stir in ham mixture and cheese and pour into crust. Bake for 40 minutes or until lightly browned and set. Cool for10 minutes then serve with a green salad.

**Recipe 16**

## Mackerel Fish Cakes

**Prep:** 20 mins, **Cook:** 15 mins

- **Ingredients**
- 
- 100g tinned mackerel fillets
- 350g tinned new potatoes
- 75g tinned whole green beans
- 75g tinned sweetcorn
- Knob of butter for mash
- Olive oil for frying
- Salt and pepper to taste
- 

**Method:**

Warm through the potatoes in a pan on the hob for around five minutes. Do not boil.
Mash the potatoes and add a knob of butter and salt and pepper to taste.
Carefully mix in the sweetcorn and pre-chopped whole green beans.
Take the mixture and form it into circular cakes with your hands. Put them into the fridge for half an hour to firm up.
Warm a little olive oil into a non- stick pan and place the fish cakes into the pan to fry, about 5 minutes on each side.
Cook on a medium heat and remove when golden.
Serve with a wedge of fresh lemon.

**Recipe 17**

## Leftover chicken Recipe

Prep 20 mins. Cook 30 mins. Serves 4

**Ingredients**

500g potatoes

350g chicken (cooked), shredded

1 onion, finely chopped

100g mushrooms, chopped

200g bacon, chopped

1 garlic (clove), crushed

1 tsp herbs, mixed

**For the Cheese sauce**

40g butter

40g plain flour

570ml milk

100g cheddar, grated

**Method**

Preheat oven 180'C/Gas mark 4

Meanwhile boil the potatoes until tender, drain and cut into thin slices

Use half the potatoes to line a greased ovenproof dish

Lightly fry the chopped onion, mushrooms and bacon, you can use low fat bacon to make it slightly healthier - add the finely chopped garlic

Mix together with the cooked chicken and add a pinch of mixed herbs with black pepper to season

Spoon the mixture over the potato slices and top with another layer of potato slices

Just before serving add a sprinkle of low-fat cheese on the top and pop into the oven to melt

Add the cheese sauce (see below for instructions)

Pop in oven for 20-30 mins until the top is browned

**Cheese sauce**

Melt the butter in a saucepan on a low heat

Stir in the flour and cook for a couple of minutes, stirring constantly, until    you have a smooth paste

Slowly pour the milk in, stirring all the time

Bring to the boil, stirring with a balloon whisk, until thickened
Add the grated cheese to the mix and stir until melted
Use black pepper for seasoning to taste

**Recipe 18**

## Mushroom & Ham Omelette

**Serves 2**

**Prep:** 5 mins

**Cook:** 10 mins

**Ingredients**

1 chopped onion
4 Chestnut Mushrooms chopped
50g grated cheddar cheese
4 free range eggs
100g diced ham
Salt and pepper for seasoning
**Method**

Fry onion, add mushrooms and ham, stir and when reasonably cooked, add beaten eggs
Sprinkle grated cheese on top and cook until omelette has set, then serve with a green salad

**Recipe 19**

## One-pot Salmon with asparagus

Prep 10 mins

Cook 45-50 mins

Serves 2

**Ingredients**

400 g small new potatoes halved
2 tbsp olive oil
8 Asparagus spears trimmed and halved
two handfuls of cherry tomatoes halved
1 tbsp Balsamic Vinegar
2 salmon fillets approx. 140g each
handful basil leaves

**Method**

Heat oven to 220C/fan 200C/gas 7. Put the potatoes and 1 tbsp of olive oil into an ovenproof dish, then roast the potatoes for 20 mins until starting to brown, the add the asparagus in with the potatoes, then return to the oven for 15 mins.
Put in the cherry tomatoes and vinegar and nestle the salmon amongst the vegetables. Drizzle with the remaining oil and return to the oven for a final 10-15 mins until the salmon is cooked. Scatter over the basil leaves and serve everything scooped straight from the dish.

**Recipe 20**

## Parmesan Flavoured Chicken

**Prep** 25 mins. **Cook** 20 mins. Serves 2

- **Ingredients**
- 
- 20g (4 tsp) Parmesan, finely grated
- 1 tsp plain flour
- salt and freshly ground black pepper
- 1 egg
- 2 × 150g skinless chicken breasts, halved
- 70g peas, fresh or frozen
- 50g baby spinach leaves
- 1 tsp extra virgin olive oil
- 1 tsp white wine vinegar
- 
- **Method**
- 
- Preheat the grill to a medium setting. Loosely mix the Parmesan, flour and a little salt and pepper on a plate. Beat the egg in a wide bowl.
- Dip each piece of chicken first in the egg and then in the Parmesan, making sure it is lightly coated on both sides.
- Place the chicken pieces on a grill tray and cook under the grill for 5–6 minutes on each side until golden and cooked through. While the chicken is cooking, cook the peas in boiling water for 6 minutes until tender.
- Drain the peas and return to the pan. Stir through the spinach, allowing it to wilt slightly in the heat. Add the olive oil and vinegar and stir through.

- Transfer to 2 serving plates and arrange 2 pieces of chicken each on top of the green vegetables.

Recipe 21

## Potato Roti with fried Egg

Prep & cook time, less than 30 mins

Serves: 4

**Ingredients:**

1 tbsp butter
Good dash olive oil
400g **cooked** potatoes, quartered
1 red onion, sliced
2 tbsp capers
125g black olives, pitted and sliced
2 tbsp breadcrumbs
50gram parmesan shavings
Poached eggs, optional

**Method:**

Melt butter and oil on BBQ plate.
Fry potatoes with onion, capers and olives, tossing until potatoes just begin to brown.
Add breadcrumbs to absorb the oil and give nice crispy finish.
Heat a second frying pan with a dash of olive oil and fry the eggs
Plate Roti and place the egg on top.

**Recipe 22**

## Portobello Mushroom Muffins with Wedge Chips

Prep 15 Mins. Cook 30 Mins. Serves 4

- **Ingredients**
- 
- 4 Portello Mushrooms, stems removed
- 4 slices Cheddar Cheese
- 4tbsp olive oil
- 3 medium potatoes cut into wedges
- 2 tbsp chopped parsley
- 2 tbsp mayonnaise
- 2 tbsp French mustard
- Salt & pepper to taste
- Lettuce & sliced red onion for serving
- 4 Muffins halved, toasted and buttered
- 

**Method**

Heat oven to 220C/Gas Mark 7. Rub the mushrooms with 2 tablespoons of oil, and salt and pepper and put on an oven tray stem-side down and roast for 15-20 mins until tender. Top each mushroom with a slice of Cheddar and continue to cook for 3-5 mins more until melted.

Meanwhile, on a separate oven tray toss the potatoes with the remaining 2 tablespoons of oil and season with salt and pepper. Roast for 18-20 mins turning once, until tender, then sprinkle with the parsley.

Mix together the mayonnaise and mustard in a small bowl.

Spread the muffins with the mayonnaise, then stack the lettuce, mushrooms and onion, between the muffins. Serve with the wedges.

**Recipe 23**

## Salmon with beetroot and feta salsa

Prep 10 mins.
Cook 15 mins.
Serves 2

### Ingredients

200g cooked beetroot
2 spring onions, sliced on a diagonal
2 lemons
70g feta cheese
2 skin on salmon fillets
Salt and Pepper to season

### Method

**Salsa**
Chop the beetroot and feta into small cubes and mix with the juice and zest of 1 lemon and salt and pepper.

**Salmon**
Season the salmon. Heat 2 tbsp of oil in a non-stick frying pan over a high heat. When hot add the salmon, skin-side down, and cook for 3 mins. Flip over, turn the heat down and cook for a further 4-5 mins.
Serve with the beetroot salsa and the remaining lemon, cut into wedges

**Recipe 24**

## Tomato Salsa Accompaniment

Prep 15 mins.  No cook. Serves 6

**Ingredients:**

6 firm red tomatoes
1 red onion
1 bunch fresh basil

**Dressing:**

2–3 tbsp mayonnaise
2 tbsp quality olive oil
Salt and pepper to taste

**Method:**

Cut tomatoes into small squares.
Finely dice red onion.
Finely cut fresh basil.
Place all ingredients into a serving bowl together.
In a separate bowl drizzle olive oil into mayonnaise, a small amount at a time until you have a runny consistency.
Gently fold the dressing into the tomato salsa, and season with salt and pepper.
Suggestion:
Prepare the tomato salsa just before serving your main meal.
Goes well with Chicken, BBQ meats, or a full English breakfast

**Recipe 25**

## Tuna Patties on Crumpets

Prep 10 mins.
Cook 10 mins.
Serves 4

### Ingredients

425g tuna (tinned in spring water)
1 onion, diced
4 tbsp mayonnaise
½ tbsp of curry powder or four crushed garlic cloves
1 egg
25g grated cheese
2 tbsp breadcrumbs
4 large round crumpets

### Method:

Place all ingredients except the crumpets in a large bowl.
Mix together, then shape into 4 cakes, then roll in breadcrumbs on a separate plate.
Cook patties on either a BBQ or shallow fry in a frying pan
Serve on hot buttered crumpets
Suggestion:
With side salad or a sweet chilli sauce dip or the Tomato Salsa Accompaniment

Recipe 26

## Vegetarian fresh Saag Paneer

Prep 20 mins. Cook 20 mins. Serves 4

- **Ingredients**
- 1 tbsp olive oil
- 250g Paneer Cheese cut into cubes
- 1 onion, chopped
- 1 thumb-sized piece of ginger, peeled and cut into matchsticks
- 2 cloves garlic, finely sliced
- 1 fresh green chilli, de-seeded and sliced
- 1 tsp tomato purée
- 200g cherry tomatoes, halved
- 1 tsp ground coriander
- 1 tsp ground cumin
- ¼ tsp ground turmeric
- 1 tsp mild chilli powder
- 200g fresh spinach leaves
- Salt and freshly ground black pepper
- 
- **Method**
- Heat the oil in a wide lidded frying pan over a high heat. Add the paneer cubes and season generously. Fry for a few minutes until golden, stirring often. Remove from the pan and set aside.
- Reduce the heat and add the onion. Fry for 5 minutes before adding the ginger, garlic and chilli. Fry for another 5 minutes. Add the tomato purée and cherry tomatoes. Put the lid on and cook for 5–7 minutes.

- Add all the spices and a little more salt. Return the paneer to the pan and stir until coated. Then add the spinach leaves and return the lid to the pan. Allow the spinach to wilt for 2–3 minutes and then stir into the sauce

**Recipe 27**

**Vegetarian Wrap**

Prep 40 mins. Cook 45 mins. Serves 4

**Ingredients:**
6-8 wholemeal wraps
Half a bunch basil leaves, roughly chopped
1 handful pine nuts, toasted
1 bunch parsley
250g pumpkin, cubed
1 packet of rocket or baby spinach leaves
2-3 tomatoes, diced
1 tbsp olive oil for frying

**Dressing:**
2 tbsp lemon juice
1 tbsp olive oil
½ garlic clove, crushed

**Method:**
Fill a saucepan half full of water.
Add the pumpkin and cook on the hob until almost soft (alternatively microwave the pumpkin).
Preheat frying pan with olive oil.
Add the cooked pumpkin to the frying pan and fry until golden brown.
Place all remaining ingredients together in a mixing bowl and mix well, then add the pumpkin and combine.
To prepare dressing.
Mix all the ingredients together in a small bowl.

Put the filling on the wraps and add the dressing.
Roll up the wrap and serve.
**Tip**
These can be stored in the fridge for up to three days.

## Dinner recipes

1. Baked Bean Casserole
2. Camp Beef Casserole
3. Camp Kitchen Pan Chicken
4. Cheese Base Pizza
5. Cheesy Beef & Baked Bean Cottage Pie
6. Chicken Rolls in Tomato Sauce
7. Chicken Tamale Pie
8. Chilli Con Carne
9. Simple Corned Beef Hash
10. Italian stuffed Chicken
11. Crispy Chicken
12. Crustless Red Onion & Courgette Quiche
13. Deep Filled Homity Pie
14. Diced Chicken & Pasta
15. Garlic Butter Salmon
16. Healthy Option Homity Pie
17. Healthy Lasagne
18. Hot Pot Curried Lamb with Red Lentils
19. Italian Beef with Tomatoes & Peppers
20. Italian Chicken
21. Lamb Pot Roast

22. Lemon & Dill Salmon One Pot
23. Macaroni Cheese & ham
24. Marinated Butterflied BBQ Lamb
25. Mediterranean & Basil Pasta One Pot
26. Mediterranean Chicken with Roast Vegetables
27. Mediterranean Chicken
28. Mediterranean Salmon Fillet
29. Mediterranean Vegetables with Lamb
30. Middle Eastern Chicken and Rice
31. Mr Posh Chicken Kiev
32. Prosciutto Salmon One Pot Wrap
33. Roast Chicken with Harissa
34. Roast Vegetables & Rosemary
35. Sausage Casserole Caravan Style
36. Slow Cooked Ham & Sweet Potato Curry
37. Slow Cooked Beef Bourguignon
38. Slow roast Lamb Shanks
39. Smoky Pork Chilli
40. Spicy Couscous Fritters
41 Spring Chicken Stew with Tarragon Butter
42 Sweet Onion Chicken
43. Garlic ChickenC
44. Teriyaki Salmon One Pot
45. Tomato Presto Salmon One Pot
46. Traditional Goulash
47. Vegetable Pocket
48. Vegetable Crumble

**Recipe 1**

**Camp fire Baked Bean Casserole**

Prep 15 mins.
Cook 30 mins.
Serves 4

**Ingredients**

400g tin baked beans
250 g chopped ham
1 onion chopped
4 eggs
1 crushed garlic clove
25g grated carrot
75g grated courgette
50g grated cheese
Salt and pepper to taste

**Method**

Cover the bottom of the pan with a layer of baked beans, add the courgette, carrot, onion and garlic, then layer with ham and cheese
Crack the eggs into a jug and beat, then pour over the contents of the pan
      Cook in a camp oven for 30 minutes.

**Cooks tip**
If you don't have a grater slice the carrots very thinly, otherwise they will not cook through, and cut the cheese very thinly and lay over the ham.

**Recipe 2**

## Camp fire Beef Casserole

Prep 15 mins. Cook approx. 90 mins. Serves 4

**Ingredients:**
2 tbsp oil
1kg rump steak, cubed
2 tbsp flour
1 large onion, finely chopped
1 clove garlic
350mls beef stock (Beef cube)
1 tsp tomato puree
1 bay leaf
¼ tsp marjoram or oregano
500g potatoes, quartered
2 large carrots, cut into 2" lengths and then halved
150g mushrooms, halved
2 tbsp parsley chopped, or use 1 tbsp dried

Method:
Place the meat and flour in a plastic bag and shake to coat. If you want to add heat add a teaspoon of paprika
Heat the oil in a frying pan or camp oven and brown the meat, making sure to turn it so it browns all over.
Once browned add all other ingredients except the vegetables and cook for 50 mins.
Add vegetables and cook for further 30/40 minutes until everything is tender. If the gravy is not thick enough remove lid and cook until you have thick gravy.
Season to your taste with salt and pepper

**Recipe 3**

## Camp Kitchen Pan Chicken

Prep 20 mins.
Cook 90 mins.
Serves 4

- **Ingredients**

- 

- Splash of Olive oil

- 1 large onion diced

- 500g diced chicken breast or thigh

- 2 tsp hot chilli powder or to taste

- 2 tsp turmeric

- 4 cloves crushed garlic

- Salt and Pepper

- 4 carrots diced

- 4 large potatoes diced

- 1 large tin chopped tomato

- 1 tin chickpeas

- 125ml water

- Handful of dried mint leaves

- ½ bunch parsley chopped (adds flavour)

- ½ bunch mint leaves chopped (adds flavour)
- A squeeze of lemon or lime juice, again to flavour
- 
- **Method**
- 
- In a large camp oven or deep sided pan, heat the oil, then add the onion and the chicken, browning the chicken all over.
- Add chilli powder, turmeric, garlic, salt & pepper, and stir until fragrant, then add the carrot and potatoes.
- Stir until the veg is fully coated.
- Add the tin of chopped tomatoes, chickpeas, water, and the dried mint leaves, slowly stirring until combined. Bring it all to a simmer, then cover and cook on a slow simmer for 90 minutes.
- Fold through fresh parsley and mint leaves and cook for 5 more minutes.
- Squeeze lemon or lime juice on top then serve.
- Note
- Serve in a bowl on its own or on a bed of cooked rice. (see the chapter Basic Cook for a rice recipe)

**Recipe 4**

## Cheese based Pizza

Prep 30 mins Cook 15-20 mins. **Ingredients**
**For the base**
250g self-raising flour
60g grated cheese
150ml milk
35g butter

**For the topping**
2-3 slices of diced cooked ham
3 chestnut mushrooms sliced
Tomato puree (enough to spread thinly on base)
25g garlic butter melted (Lurpak)
100g Mozzarella (or cheat and use cheddar)
Fresh basil (optional)

**Method**
Preheat the oven to 220°C/425°F/Gas mark 7
**For the base** (to make see Basic Cook)
Mix the flour, milk cheese and butter in a bowl - it should come together as a dough
Flour your work surface and putting the dough on it knead it lightly to bring all the bits together and work the butter and milk right through it. Roll the dough out to a 10-inch pizza size and place it on a floured baking tray
**For the topping**
Rub the liquid garlic butter onto the pizza and spread it thinly to within 2cm of the edge, then spread the tomato puree over the pizza base, sprinkle the cheese evenly then add the ham and mushrooms to taste.
Finally, sprinkle the herbs and add a drizzle of olive oil.
Bake for 10-15 minutes (or longer), until the cheese has fully melted, and the pizza is crispy.

**Recipe 5**

## Cheesy Beef & Baked Bean Cottage Pie

Prep 10 mins. Cook 40 mins. Serves 6

### Ingredients:

1 tbsp olive oil

1 onion, finely diced

1 carrot, chopped

2 tsp curry powder

2 tsp cumin seeds

20g parsley, chopped

500g beef mince

1 x 415g  tin baked beans

2 tbsp Worcestershire sauce

1 tbsp flour

125 ml beef stock

Salt and pepper to taste

300g mashed potato for topping (see basic cook)

100g grated cheese

**Method:**

Preheat the oven to bake at 200°C/180F/Gas mark 6

Heat the oil in a frying pan on medium heat.

Add the onion, carrot, curry powder and cumin seeds.

Cook for 5 minutes stirring frequently.

Turn the heat to high before adding the mince.

Fry the meat for 6-8 minutes breaking apart with back of spoon until browned all over.

Stir in the Worcestershire sauce, flour and stock and mix well before adding the baked beans.

Continue cooking for 8 minutes until the sauce has thickened.

Add chopped parsley.

Season with salt and pepper to taste.

Pour into a baking dish and top with mashed potato and grated cheese.

Bake until lightly golden and lightly bubbling for approximately 20-30 minutes.

Suggestion

This dish can be prepared at home up to two days before it is baked and put in a rectangular Pyrex dish.

Serve with dinner rolls or Brown seeded bread (Hovis)

**Recipe 6**

## Chicken rolls in Tomato sauce

Slow cooker, Prep 15mins.
Ready in 3 hours (oven) 6 hrs. (slow cooker), Serves 4

- **Ingredients**
- 100g sausage meat
- 4 skinless, boneless chicken thighs, about 370g
- 1 onion, peeled and chopped
- 2 garlic cloves, peeled and finely chopped)
- 1 red pepper, deseeded and roughly chopped
- 1 green pepper, deseeded and roughly chopped
- 1 × 400g can butter beans, rinsed and drained
- 1 × 400g can chopped tomatoes
- ½ chicken stock cube
- 1 tsp dried oregano
- 

**Method**

Preheat the oven to 140C/120C fan/Gas Mark 2 if using the oven.

Divide the sausage meat into roughly 4 equal portions. Open the chicken thighs and lay them flat. Place the portion of sausage meat in the middle of the chicken and pull up the sides so that the meat is enclosed in a tight roll. If you wish to make a neater parcel you can hold the two ends of the chicken together with a cocktail stick. Turn the chicken roll over so that the join is on the bottom, or alternatively wrap in Parma ham (this will add more taste and hold the chicken wrap tightly).

Use a large casserole dish or slow cooker. Layer the onion, garlic and peppers at the base of the dish, then add the butter beans. Place the stuffed chicken thighs on top and pour on the chopped tomatoes. Crunch up the stock cube in your fingers and sprinkle over the top. Add the oregano. Finally, top up with 300ml of water until the chicken is generously covered.

Cook in the oven for 3 hours. Alternatively, cook in the slow cooker for at least 6 hours.

**Recipe 7**

## Chicken Tamale Pie

Prep 5 mins, Cook 40 mins

- **Ingredients**
- 
- 350g diced cooked chicken
- 375g prepared salsa (see chapter basic cook)
- 1 x425g tin black beans, drained and rinsed
- 375g chicken broth
- 1 tablespoon chilli powder
- 2 spring onions (white and green parts), sliced
- 100g cornflour
- 100g grated mature Cheddar cheese
- 1 tablespoon unsalted butter
- Salt and freshly ground black pepper
  - Sour cream, for serving

**Method**

Preheat the oven to 200c/Gas mark 6. Heat the chicken, salsa, beans, half of the broth and the chilli powder in an ovenproof skillet over medium heat, stirring, until simmering. Stir in the spring onions and remove from the heat.

Meanwhile, combine the cornflour with the remaining broth and 250ml of water in a medium pan. Bring to a simmer over a medium heat stirring until very thick, about 5 to 7 minutes. Remove from the heat and stir in the cheese and butter. Season with salt and pepper.

Spread the cornflour mixture over the filling and bake until cooked through, about 30 minutes, then stand for 15 minutes. Serve with the sour cream.

**Recipe 8**

# Chilli con carne

**Prep** 10 mins.
**Cook** 45 mins.
Serves 4-6

- **Ingredients**
-
- 500g lean minced beef, (5% fat)
- 1 onion, peeled and chopped
- ½ teaspoon chilli powder, or less to taste
- 400g chopped tomatoes
- 400g kidney beans, well washed and drained
- 2 crushed garlic cloves
- 1 tsp paprika
- 1 tsp dried oregano
- 150ml beef stock
- Fresh coriander, to garnish
-

## Method

Dry fry the minced beef and onion together in a large frying pan over a medium heat for 10 minutes, or until the meat is browned and the onion softened
Add the garlic, chilli, paprika and oregano and fry for 2-3 minutes. Stir in the chopped tomatoes. Pour in the beef stock and stir through the red kidney beans
Bring the mixture up to the boil, stirring occasionally, then reduce the heat to a simmer. Season to taste, then leave to cook for 30 minutes. Garnish with fresh coriander to serve.

**Recipe 9**

## Simple Corned beef hash

**Prep** 5 mins
**Cook** 30 mins
Serves 2

### Ingredients

300g tin corned beef
350g tin new potatoes
Knob of butter for mash
Salt and pepper to taste

### Method

Warm the potatoes in a pan on the hob for around five minutes.
Drain potatoes
Add a knob of butter as well as salt and pepper and roughly mash.
Chop the corned beef into small cubes and carefully fold into the mash
Spoon the mixture into a casserole dish and pop into a pre-heated oven on a medium to high heat for around 30 minutes or until golden brown.
You could add 100g of grated cheese as a topping 10 minutes before the end of cooking time to get that moreish flavour

Recipe 10

## Italian Stuffed Chicken

**Prep** 20 mins. **Cook** 25-30 mins. Serves 4

### Ingredients

4 30cm x 30cm pieces of non-stick foil
4 boneless skinless chicken breasts
2 tbsp. extra-virgin olive oil
Salt & black pepper
1 tsp. Italian seasoning
1 courgette halved and thinly sliced into half rounds
3 medium tomatoes halved and thinly sliced into rounds
2 yellow peppers, thinly sliced
1/2 red onion, thinly sliced
110g shredded mozzarella

### Method

Preheat oven to 200c/Gas Mark 6. Place the raw chicken on a cutting board and make a slit in each breast, (making a pocket) being careful not to cut through completely. Drizzle the oil over the chicken and season with salt, pepper, and Italian seasoning.
Stuff each chicken breast with courgette, tomato, pepper, and red onion.
Sprinkle each chicken breast with mozzarella.
Wrap each breast in foil and fold over the top to make an envelope
Bake for approx. 25-30 minutes until the chicken is cooked through and no longer pink.

Open the top of the tin foil envelope carefully and brown for 5-8 minutes
Serve.

## Crispy Chicken

### With Buttered Cabbage & Mashed Potatoes

Prep 20 mins.

Cook 60 mins.

Serves 4

### Ingredients

125ml Dijon mustard

¼ teaspoon black pepper

2 tablespoons extra-virgin olive oil

1 teaspoon low-salt

6 skinless, bone-in chicken thighs (about 1 kilo.)

125g panko breadcrumbs

### For the cabbage

1 Savoy cabbage stem removed, chopped and shredded (about 225g.)

2 to 4 tablespoons of butter and one extra knob of butter

**Ingredients for the mashed potatoes**

900g baking potatoes, peeled and quartered

2 tablespoons butter

240ml milk, or as needed

salt and pepper to taste

**Method**

Preheat oven to 200c/Gas Mark7. Stir together the mustard, pepper, 1 tablespoon of the oil, and ¾ teaspoon of the salt in a small bowl. Brush evenly over both sides of the chicken. Place the panko in a shallow dish and dip the chicken in the breadcrumbs and place in a single layer on a wire rack set on an aluminium foil-lined oven tray. Bake for about 30 minutes or until cooked through, then let them stand for 5 minutes.

Meanwhile bring a saucepan of salted water to the boil. Add the peeled and quartered potatoes and cook for about 15 minutes until tender but still firm, then drain.

In a small saucepan heat the butter and milk over a low heat until the butter has melted, then using a potato masher or electric beater, slowly blend the milk mixture into the potatoes until smooth and creamy. Season with salt and pepper to taste.

Remove all the tough outer leaves from the cabbage. Cut the cabbage into four, remove the stalk and then cut each quarter into fine shreds, working across the grain. Put 3 tablespoons of water into a wide saucepan, together with the butter and a pinch of salt. Bring to a boil, add the cabbage and stir in over a high heat, then cover the saucepan and cook for a few minutes. Stir again and add some salt to taste, freshly ground pepper and the knob of butter. Serve immediately.

Serve with the chicken and mashed potatoes.

**Recipe 12**

## Crustless red onion and courgette quiche

**Prep** 20 mins.
**Cook** 40 mins.
Serves 4

### Ingredients

2 courgettes
Low calorie cooking spray
2 red onions halved and finely sliced
1 green chilli (mild) deseeded and finely chopped
100g low fat natural cottage cheese
6 large eggs
1tsp dried mixed herbs
Small handful of finely chopped fresh mint

### Method

Preheat the oven to 180c/Gas Mark 4. Coarsely grate the courgettes and place in a large sieve. Press down to remove as much liquid as possible and set aside.
Spray a large frying pan with low calorie cooking spray and place over a medium heat. Add the onions, courgettes and chilli and stir-fry for 10 minutes. Season to taste and transfer to the prepared baking dish, spreading evenly across the base. Spread the cottage cheese over the vegetable mixture.
Beat the eggs in a bowl, season and add the dried herbs and mint. Pour the egg mixture over the cottage cheese. Place in the oven and cook for 30 minutes or until set and golden. Remove from the oven and allow to rest for about 15

minutes before cutting into wedges. This can be eaten warm or cold. If serving cold, cool, cover and chill until ready to eat.

**Recipe 14**

# Diced Chicken and Pasta

Prep 15 mins.
Cook 45 mins.
Serves 4

**Ingredients:**
- 500g chicken breast, diced
- 1 tbsp oil
- 1 tbsp Italian seasoning
- 375g fettuccini pasta
- 200g of Fusilli pasta
- 1 avocado, diced
- 250g cherry tomatoes, halved
- 50-100g semi sun dried tomatoes, sliced
- 1 tbsp lemon juice
-
- **Method:**
- Sprinkle Italian seasoning on diced chicken, then brown in a wok or large frying pan.
- Cook pasta in saucepan as per the packet directions. (Normally in boiling water for 11 minutes)
- Add halved tomatoes, sliced sun-dried tomatoes and diced avocado to wok or frying pan and cook until chicken is cooked through.
- Drain pasta and add to the chicken.
- Mix well. You might wish to add about ⅓ cup of the pasta water to ensure meal retains some moisture.
- Add lemon juice to desired taste.
- **Suggestion**

- Vegetable variations: use any vegetables you have available at time of cooking. I have used carrot, broccoli and red, green or yellow peppers

Recipe 15

## Garlic Butter Salmon one pot

Servings: 1, Cook time 30/35 minutes, Prep time 10 minutes

- **Ingredients**
- 
- Aluminium foil, 12x18 inches (30cm x45cm)
- 1 white potato, thinly sliced
- 6 individual green beans sliced long ways
- Salt & pepper to taste
- 6 ounces skinless salmon, If the Salmon was bought frozen allow a minimum of two hours to defrost before using
- 3 tablespoons butter, melted (or use 50g of garlic butter)
- 1 clove garlic (Or if using Garlic Butter disregard the clove)
- 2 tablespoons fresh parsley, chopped or dried parsley
- 
- **Method**
- 
- Preheat oven to 350°F/180°C. Gas Mark 5
- Fold the Foil in half, then open.
- In a bowl, combine the butter, garlic, and parsley.
- On one half of the foil, lay down the potatoes 7 green beans. Drizzle on half of the garlic butter mixture. Add salt and pepper as desired.
- Lay the salmon on the potatoes 7 green beans and drizzle the remaining garlic butter. Add salt and pepper as desired.
- Fold the foil over the salmon and close the foil together by folding it over itself along the edges.
- Bake for 25/30 minutes.

**Recipe 16**

# Homity pie (Healthy option)

Prep 20 mins. Cook 40 mins. Serves 4

- **Ingredients**
-
- Low calorie cooking spray
- 340g potatoes, peeled and cubed
- 225g onions, chopped
- 225g leeks, thinly sliced
- 198g frozen peas
- 2 garlic cloves, finely chopped
- A handful of fresh parsley, chopped
- A handful of fresh thyme, chopped
- 2 eggs, lightly beaten
- 85ml of vegetable stock
- 160g reduced-fat Cheddar cheese, grated
- Salt and freshly ground black pepper
-
- **Method**
-
- Preheat your oven to 220°C/425°F/Gas Mark 7. Spray a medium-sized ovenproof dish with low calorie cooking spray.
- Boil potatoes for 15-20 minutes, or until tender. Drain return to the pan and mash. Set aside until needed.
- Spray a large non-stick frying pan with low calorie cooking spray and stir-fry the onions, leeks and peas over a medium heat for 6-8 minutes, or until the vegetables have softened.

- Add the mashed potatoes, garlic, parsley, thyme eggs, stock and half the cheese, season and stir to combine. Spoon the mixture into the prepared ovenproof dish and scatter over the remaining cheese. Bake for 20 minutes or until golden.

**Recipe 17**

## Healthy lasagne

Prep 40 mins.
Cook 2 hrs.
Serves 6

- **Ingredients**
-
- 500g lean minced beef
- 2 onions, finely chopped
- 2 celery sticks, trimmed and chopped
- 3 garlic cloves, peeled and crushed
- 2 large carrots, peeled and grated
- 400g tin chopped tomatoes
- 400ml hot beef stock
- 3 bay leaves
- 1 tsp black peppercorns
- 550ml semi-skimmed milk
- 3 tbsp cornflour
- 2 tsp Dijon mustard
- ¼ whole nutmeg, freshly grated
- 2 large courgettes, (or one leek see note) very thinly sliced lengthways (approx. 2-3mm thick)
- 4 vine tomatoes, sliced
- 40g mature Cheddar, coarsely grated
- 20g Parmesan, finely grated
- green salad or green vegetables to serve

## Method

Preheat the oven to 200°C/fan 180°/Gas Mark 6. Heat a large non-stick heavy-bottomed saucepan, add the mince, season well and fry over a medium-high heat for 5 mins, stirring frequently until golden brown. Add half the chopped onions and the celery and season. Fry over a medium heat for 5-6 mins or until softened. Add the garlic and fry for another minute. Add the grated carrots and fry for 3-4 mins.

Next add the tinned tomatoes, stock, and one of the bay leaves and bring to the boil. Cover with a lid, turn down the heat to medium-low and leave to simmer for 25 mins, stirring occasionally. Remove the lid and simmer for another 15 mins or until the sauce has thickened slightly.

While the mince is cooking, put the rest of the onion in a saucepan with the remaining bay leaves, peppercorns and the milk (reserving 3 tbsp) and place over a low heat. Bring to a gentle simmer and cook for 2-3 mins. Remove from the heat and leave the milk to infuse for 10 mins. Drain through a sieve retain the liquid (Infused Milk) and discard the bay leaf, onion and peppercorns.

Put the cornflour in a small bowl, add the reserved milk and whisk to a thick paste. Add to the infused milk, and place over a low heat and simmer, stirring frequently for 5 mins or until thickened. Add the mustard and grated nutmeg and season well, adding a little more milk if the sauce is too thick

Blanch the courgette slices in a large pan of boiling salted water for 1 min, remove from the boiling water with tongs and drain well on kitchen paper. (It's important to get rid of as much water as possible at this stage or the lasagne will be very watery.)

Spoon half of the mince mixture into a lasagne dish. Top with an even layer of blanched courgettes, then season well. Repeat with the rest of the mince and finish with the rest of the courgettes. Pour the white sauce over the top and place the sliced tomatoes in lines on the top. Mix the Cheddar and Parmesan cheeses and sprinkle over the top. Bake for 30 mins or until golden-brown and bubbling.

Divide between 6 plates and serve with green salad or greens.

**Note** if using Leeks instead of courgettes cut 5mm off the bottom and the top green foliage and cut length ways one skin at a time, warm before use.

# Hot pot curried lamb with red lentils

Prep Less than 30 mins. Cook 2-3hrs. Serves 4

- **Ingredients**
- 4 lamb leg steaks, cut into 3cm chunks
- 3 onions, peeled and sliced
- 2 tbsp sunflower oil
- 4 large garlic cloves, sliced
- 40g fresh ginger, grated
- 4 fresh chillies, de-seeded and sliced (or dried Chilli powder)
- 40g tikka curry spice
- 150g red lentils
- 4 large tomatoes, roughly chopped (or a 415 g tin chopped tomatoes)
- 15g fresh chopped coriander (or dried coriander)
- 400ml water
- 

- **Method**
- Place the lamb into a bowl with 10g of the tikka curry spice and mix well until evenly coated
- In a casserole dish add 1 tablespoon of the sunflower oil and gently cook the onions over a medium-low heat until they soften. Add the garlic, chilli, ginger and remaining tikka curry spice, reduce the heat, and continue cooking for about 5 minutes
- Add the chopped tomatoes, lentils, water and season with a pinch of salt and black pepper, and bring to a simmer
- Meanwhile, heat the remaining oil in a frying pan and cook the lamb until sealed all over. Transfer to the casserole pot and give everything a good stir, then cover with a lid and leave to simmer, stirring occasionally, for 2-3 hours on a low heat

- Once the lamb is cooked through and tender, taste the sauce and adjust seasoning if required. Stir through the fresh coriander if using) and serve immediately

**Recipe 19**

## Italian Beef with Tomatoes & Peppers

Prep 20 mins.
Ready in 40 mins.
Serves 2

### Ingredients

1 tsp sunflower oil
200g lean beef strips
salt and freshly ground black pepper
½ onion, peeled and sliced into half rings
1 garlic clove, peeled and thinly sliced
½ green pepper, deseeded and sliced
½ yellow pepper, deseeded and sliced
1 × 400g tin chopped tomatoes
½ tsp dried mixed herbs
a little fresh oregano (optional)
12 large black olives, pitted (optional)

### Method

Heat the oil in a large pan over a high heat. Season the beef with salt and pepper. When the oil is hot, place in the beef and stir-fry for 2 minutes. Remove the beef from the pan and set aside.
Reduce the heat to medium and fry the onion, garlic and peppers for 5–10 minutes until tender. With the heat still at medium, add the tomatoes and herbs and simmer

for 15 minutes. Stir through the beef strips and olives (if using) and heat for a further 2 minutes before serving

**Recipe 20**

## Italian Chicken.

Prep 15 mins. Cook 30-60 mins. Serves 2

**Ingredients**

- 2 large chicken breasts, thickly sliced
- 1 tbsp oil
- 1 large onion, finely sliced
- I clove garlic, crushed
- 2 tins chopped tomatoes with basil
- Oregano to taste (optional)
- 118ml red wine (optional) or use stock or water
- Grated cheddar or parmesan cheese
- Salt and pepper to season
- 200g uncooked Fusilli pasta
- 
- **Method:**
- 
- In a large non-stick pan, sauté the onions and garlic until soft.
- Add sliced chicken and brown.
- Add the tinned tomatoes, dried herbs (if wished) and red wine and stir well until combined.
- Turn down heat and simmer for 10 minutes.
- In a separate saucepan bring water to the boil and add the pasta. Cook until just soft set timer for 11 minutes after which take it out and drain pan.

- Add the chicken mix to the pasta, stir together then serve
- Suggestion
- Serve in large bowls with the Italian Chicken on top and garnish with grated cheese or parmesan

Recipe 21

## Lamb Pot Roast

Prep 30 mins. Cook 2-3 hrs. or 7-8 hours in the slow cooker. Serves 4

### Ingredients

4 × 90g lean lamb leg steaks
2 tsp turmeric
2 tsp English mustard
1 tsp sugar
Salt and freshly ground black pepper
1 tbsp vegetable oil
1 medium onion, peeled and chopped
4 garlic cloves, peeled and chopped
1 medium sweet potato, peeled and cut into large chunks
1 × 400g tin whole tomatoes
1 × 400g tin chickpeas, rinsed and drained
500ml lamb or chicken stock (made from 1 stock cube)
100g spinach, fresh or frozen (about 4 cubes)
100g peas, fresh

### Method

Rub the lamb all over with the turmeric, mustard, sugar and salt and pepper.
In a casserole dish, heat the vegetable oil until it is smoking hot. Place the lamb in and fry for 2 minutes each side. Reduce the heat and stir in the onion and garlic and fry gently for 2 minutes.
Add the sweet potato, tomatoes, chickpeas and stock, then stir and put the lid on.
In the oven: Preheat the oven to 180C/160C fan/Gas Mark 4 and cook for 2 hours.

Stir in the spinach and peas. Replace onto the hob, bring to a gentle simmer and cook for 10 minutes. Then turn to high and cook uncovered for 30 minutes

In the slow cooker: Cook on low for 7–8 hours. Stir in the spinach and peas15 minutes before cooking end time.

Recipe 22

## Lemon and Dill Salmon one pot

Prep 10 mins
Cook 20-25 mins.
Serves 1

### Ingredients

- Non-stick Aluminium foil, 12x18 inches (30cm x 45cm)
- 7 ounces asparagus sliced in half length ways
- Olive oil to taste
- Salt & pepper to taste
- 6 ounces skinless salmon. If the Salmon was bought frozen allow a minimum of two hours to defrost before using
- 3 slices white onion
- 2 slices lemon
- 1 sprig fresh dill
-

### Method

1. Preheat oven to 350°F/180°C. Gas Mark 5
2. Fold the aluminium foil in half, then open.
3. On one half, lay down the asparagus. Drizzle on oil and sprinkle on salt & pepper.

4. Lay the salmon on the asparagus, and add a little more oil, salt, and pepper.

5. Place the onion, lemon, and dill on the salmon. (If using frozen salmon allow a minimum of two hours to defrost before using)

5. Fold the foil over the salmon and close together by folding it over itself along the edges.

6. Bake for 20-25 minutes

**Recipe 23**

## Macaroni cheese and Ham

Prep time 10 mins
Cook time 35 mins
Serves: 6

### Ingredients

50g   butter or if you want add Garlic butter instead. (Local supermarket)
1 small onion, finely chopped
1 ½tablespoons plain flour
1 teaspoon salt
750ml skimmed milk
225g uncooked macaroni
175g grated mature Cheddar cheese
200g tin of chopped ham (chop the chopped ham into 10cm cubes)

### Method

Melt the butter in a saucepan pan over medium heat. Add the onion and cook until soft, then stir in the flour and salt.

Add the milk and macaroni to the saucepan and bring to the boil. Reduce the heat and cover. Simmer for 10 minutes, stirring occasionally.

Add the chopped ham and stir in leaving to simmer for 5 minutes or until the pasta is tender.

Finally add the cheese and stir until it melts.
Serve and enjoy.

**Recipe 24**

## Marinated Butterflied BBQ Lamb

Prep 10 mins.
Cook 60 mins.
Serves 4-6

### Ingredients

2kg boned butterflied lamb leg
3 tbsp soy sauce
125ml orange juice
Salt & pepper
4 tbsp honey
4 tbsp mint
3 tbsp oil
Garlic to taste
teriyaki sauce

### Method

Combine marinade ingredients well in clip lock bag, add lamb and marinate meat overnight
Place on rack over low/medium heat under BBQ hood for approx. 1 hour
Note: This is also successful with de-boned lamb chops.

Note
**Goes well with BBQ Peach Salsa**

**Recipe 25**

# Mediterranean & Basil Pasta One Pot

Prep 20 mins.
Cook 30 mins.
Serves 4

- **Ingredients**
- 2 red peppers, seeded and cut into chunks
- 2 red onions, cut into wedges
- 2 mild green chillies, seeded and diced
- 3 garlic cloves, coarsely chopped
- 1 tsp golden caster sugar
- 2 tbsp grated parmesan
- 2 tbsp olive oil plus extra to serve
- 1kg small ripe tomatoes quartered
- 200g Dried Pasta
- A handful of fresh Basil leaves
-
- **Method**
- To roast the veg, preheat the oven to 200C/fan 180C/Gas Mark 6. Scatter the peppers, red onions, chillies and garlic in a large roasting tin. Sprinkle with sugar, drizzle over the oil and season well with salt and pepper. Roast for 15 minutes, then toss in the tomatoes and roast for another 15 minutes until everything is starting to soften and look golden.

- While the vegetables are roasting, cook the pasta in a large pan of salted boiling water according to packet instructions, until tender but still with a bit of bite. Drain well.
- Remove the vegetables from the oven, put in the pasta and toss lightly together. Tear the basil leaves on top and sprinkle with Parmesan to serve. If you have any leftovers it makes a great cold pasta salad – just moisten with extra olive oil if needed.

**Recipe 26**

## Mediterranean chicken with roasted vegetables

Prep 15 mins.
 Cook 40 mins.
Serves 2

- **Ingredients**
-
- 250g baby new potatoes thinly sliced
- 1 large courgette, diagonally sliced
- 1 red onion, cut into wedges
- 1 yellow pepper, seeded and cut into chunks
- 6 firm plum tomatoes, halved
- 12 black olives, pitted
- 2 skinless boneless chicken breast fillets, about 150g/5oz each
- 3 tbsp olive oil
- 1 rounded tbsp green pesto

- **Method**

-
- Preheat the oven to 200C/ Gas 6/fan oven 180C. Spread the potatoes, courgette, onion, pepper and tomatoes in a shallow roasting tin and scatter over the olives. Season with salt and ground black pepper.

- Slash the flesh of each chicken breast 3-4 times using a sharp knife, then lay the chicken on top of the vegetables.
- Mix the olive oil and pesto together until well blended and spoon evenly over the chicken. Cover the tin with foil and cook for 30 minutes.
- Remove the foil from the tin. Return to the oven and cook for a further 10 minutes until the vegetables are juicy and the chicken is cooked through (the juices should run clear when pierced with a skewer).

**Recipe 27**

## Mediterranean Chicken

Prep 10 mins.
Cook 40-45 mins.
Serves 2

- **Ingredients**
- 2 × 150g skinless, boneless chicken breasts
- 1 tbsp tomato purée
- 1 tsp chopped fresh basil
- 1 tsp olive oil
- 1 garlic clove, peeled and finely sliced
- 1 × 400g tin chopped tomatoes
- a pinch of salt
- 1 tbsp red wine vinegar
- 
- 25g light feta cheese, cut into small cubes
- **Method**
- Cut each chicken breast into 2 pieces and lightly score on both sides.
- Rub the tomato purée and half the basil over the 4 pieces of chicken and leave to rest while you prepare the sauce.
- Heat the olive oil gently in a non-stick saucepan, add the garlic and fry for 1–2 minutes until just starting to brown. Add the tinned tomatoes, salt and the remaining basil and simmer over a medium heat for 10 minutes.

- Reduce the heat, add the red wine vinegar and continue to simmer gently for another 10 minutes.
- **Meanwhile**
- Preheat the grill to medium. Arrange the chicken pieces on the grill pan and grill for 7–8 minutes on each side. The chicken should be cooked through and turning golden all over.
- •Add the chicken and feta to the tomato sauce and stir in. Heat for a further 2–3 minutes, then serve.

**Recipe 28**

## Mediterranean Salmon Fillet- With Black pitted olives

Prep 15 mins. Cook 25 mins. Serves 6

**Ingredients**

- 
  - 1 whole salmon fillet, about 800g, skin-on and trimmed
  - 9 marinated sundried tomatoes, halved
  - 18 black olives, pitted
  - 18 basil leaves
  - 3 tbsp olive oil
  - **Method**
  - 
  - Heat oven to 200C/fan 180C/gas 6. Lay the salmon on a chopping board and, using an apple corer, make 18 holes in rows of three in the salmon fillet, just going down to the skin, but not cutting all the way through.
  - Take a piece of sun-dried tomato and an olive and, using a basil leaf as a wrapper, roll up into a tight little parcel. Each parcel should be just big enough to plug into one of the holes.
  - As you roll each parcel, stuff them into the holes until they are all filled.
  - Place the salmon fillet on a piece of non-stick foil on a baking tray, then season with salt and pepper and drizzle with the olive oil. Roast in the oven for 20 mins until just cooked. Remove from the oven and leave to cool until

just warm, then carefully lift the salmon onto a serving dish and serve, or leave to cool completely (see tips, below).

- 
- **Recipe Tip, Use up the spare salmon**
- The salmon left over from coring the fillet can be used for making fishcakes or a fish pie. You could also make a tartare by finely chopping salmon and mixing with lemon juice, olive oil, chopped shallot and seasoning, then serving with toast.

Recipe 29

## Mediterranean Vegetables with Lamb

- Prep 15 mins.
- Cook 30 mins.
- Serves 4
- 
- **Ingredients**
- 
- 1 tbsp olive oil
- 250g lean lamb fillet, trimmed of any fat and thinly sliced
- 140g shallots, halved
- 2 large courgettes, cut into chunks
- ½ tsp each ground cumin, paprika and ground coriander
- 1 red, 1 orange and 1 green pepper, cut into chunks
- 1 garlic clove, sliced
- 150ml vegetable stock
- 250g cherry tomatoes
- handful coriander leaves, roughly chopped
- 
- **Method**
- 
- Heat the oil in a large, heavy-based frying pan. Cook the lamb and shallots over a high heat for 2-3 mins until golden. Add the courgettes and stir-fry for 3-4 mins until beginning to soften.

- Add the spices and toss well, then add the peppers and garlic. Reduce the heat and cook over a moderate heat for 4-5 mins until they start to soften.
- Pour in the stock and stir to coat. Add the tomatoes, season, then cover with a lid and simmer for 15 mins, stirring occasionally until the veg are tender. Stir through the coriander to serve.

**Recipe 30**

## Middle Eastern Chicken and Rice

Prep 10 mins. Cook Time: 30 mins. Serves 6

**Ingredients**

**Spice Mixture**
2 tsp ground allspice, plus more for later
1 tsp black pepper
3/4 tsp ground green cardamom, plus more for later
1/4 tsp ground turmeric, plus more for later

**For Chicken**

6 boneless skinless chicken thighs
Salt & Pepper to taste
Extra virgin olive oil
300g chopped yellow onions (about 1/2 large onion)
100g carrots, chopped
300g frozen peas

330g cooked chickpeas (or from canned chickpeas, drained and rinsed)

390g Basmati rice, rinsed

2 cinnamon sticks

1 dry bay leaf

475 ml boiling. low-sodium chicken broth

## Instructions

In a small bowl, mix the spices to make the spice mixture. Set aside for now.

Pat chicken thighs dry and cut them into large pieces, Season well with salt, then season with the spice mixture. Work the chicken with clean hands to make sure all the pieces are well-coated with the spice mixture. Set at room temperature for 20 minutes or so (if you have the time).

In a large and deep cooking skillet with a lid, heat 3 tbsp extra virgin olive oil on medium-high until shimmering but not smoking. Brown chicken briefly on both sides (you are not trying to fully cook the chicken at this point). Remove from skillet and set aside for now.

To the same skillet, now add onions, carrots, and frozen peas. Cook for 4 minutes or so, tossing regularly, until tender. Add chickpeas and rice. Season with salt, 1/2 tsp allspice and 1/4 tsp ground cardamom. Stir to combine.

Add chicken back to the skillet (nestle the pieces in between the rice). Add cinnamon sticks, bay leaf, and chicken broth. Bring to a boil.

Turn heat to low. Cover and cook for 20 minutes or until fully cooked.

Remove from heat, garnish with parsley and serve with a side salad

**Recipe 31**

## Mr. Posh Chicken Kiev

Prep 15 mins
Cook 25-30 mins.
Serves 2

### Ingredients

½ tsp olive oil
1 garlic clove, peeled and very finely chopped
2 tbsp extra-light cream cheese
2 × 150g (5oz) skinless, boneless chicken breasts
2 slices Parma ham (prosciutto)

### Method

Preheat the oven to 200C/fan 180C/Gas Mark 6.
Heat the olive oil in a small frying pan and gently fry the garlic for 1–2 minutes until starting to brown. Remove from the heat and stir in the cream cheese.
Prepare the chicken by making a slit down one side of the chicken breast to make a pocket, then fill each pocket equally with the garlicky cream cheese

mixture. (This can get messy!) Wrap each chicken breast with a slice of Parma ham (prosciutto) and put onto a baking sheet. Cook in the oven for 20–25 minutes or until the chicken is thoroughly cooked.

Serve immediately with vegetables or a salad.

**Recipe 32**

## Prosciutto Salmon One Pot Wrap

Prep 15 mins.
Cook 25–30 mins.
Serves 1

- **Ingredients**
- Non-stick aluminium foil, 12x18 inches
- 1 small potato, thinly sliced
- 75g green beans sliced
- 30 grams Lurpak garlic butter. (can be bought in Tesco or Waitrose)
- 175g Salmon (If using frozen allow a minimum of two hours to defrost before using)
- 4 slices of Ham Serrano or Prosciutto (again bought in Tesco or Waitrose)
- Parmesan cheese
- 

**Method**

Preheat oven to 180°C/Gas Mark 5
Fold the foil in half, then open.
Lay your ham out side by side on one half of the foil.

place your thin potato and green beans with 10 grams of garlic butter and salt and pepper to your liking. Place your salmon on top of the vegetables, slice the remaining garlic butter and lay on top of the salmon and sprinkle the parmesan cheese to your liking.

Wrap the salmon and vegetables in the ham, then fold the foil over the salmon and close the foil together by folding it over itself along the edges.

Place on a baking tray Bake for 25-30 minutes.

Be careful when unwrapping your foil because of the hot steam.

**Recipe 33**

## Roasted Chicken with Harissa

Prep 10 mins.
Ready in 30 mins, plus 30 mins marinating
Serves 1

### Ingredients

1 × 150g skinless, boneless chicken breast
½ small sweet potato (75g), peeled and chopped roughly into large cubes
2 shallots, peeled and quartered
1 tbsp harissa paste (See Basic Cook)

### Method

Cut the chicken breast into 3 or 4 pieces and place in a bowl with the sweet potato and shallots.

In a small bowl, combine the harissa paste with 1 tablespoon water. Pour over the chicken and vegetables and mix thoroughly, making sure everything is coated. Cover and leave to marinate for about 30 minutes.

Preheat the oven to 220C/fan 200C/Gas Mark 7

Transfer the chicken and vegetables to a wide baking dish and cook in the oven for 25-30 minutes.

Check that the chicken is cooked through before serving

**Recipe34**

## Roasted Vegetables & Rosemary

Prep 15mins.
Cook 55mins.
Serves 2

- **Ingredients:**
- 1large carrot, halved and cut in chunks
- 1 small swede, or turnip cut in chunks
- 1 beetroot, cut into thick wedges
- 2 onions quartered
- 6 chestnut mushrooms halved
- I red pepper deseeded and cut into chunks
- 1 large sweet potato, cut into chunks
- 6 baby potatoes, halved
- 1 head garlic, broken into cloves and crushed
- 1 tsp dried rosemary
- 4Tbsp olive oil
-
- **Method:**
- Preheat oven to 200°C/Gas Mark 6.
- Line a baking tray/roasting pan with baking paper.

- Place vegetables, garlic, rosemary and the olive oil into a bowl. Toss well to coat.
- Arrange vegetables in a single layer on the prepared tray.
- Bake for 50-55 minutes, until tender and golden.
- Suggestion
- Instead of a roasting pan/oven tray use a disposable Aluminium foil roasting tray

**Recipe 35**

## Sausage Casserole Caravan style

Prep 5 mins. Cook 60 mins. Serves 4

- **Ingredients:**
- 400g can chopped tomatoes
- 250ml vegetable stock
- 8 sausages
- 4 red onions, sliced
- 1 yellow pepper, deseeded and chopped
- 1 tbsp dried basil
- 2 tsp mixed herbs
-

**Method**
- Heat oven to 220C/fan 200C/Gas mark 7.
- Put the sausages, pepper and onion into a roasting tin, then roast for 20 minutes.
- Lower oven to 200C/fan 180C/gas mark 6, then pour the tomatoes and stock over the sausages.
- Add the basil & mixed herbs, season, then stir well.
- Roast for another 20 minutes.
  - Serve with garlic bread.

- **Note**
- Sausage casserole with garlic toasts is perfect for a filling family dinner after a day of activities. It takes five minutes to prepare and 40 minutes to cook, you can pop it in the oven and go relax out in the awning while dinner cooks.
- (You can buy chopped tomatoes ready seasoned, Garlic, Basil, and so on)
- If your garlic bread is not as garlicy as you would like butter it with Lurpac garlic butter either before warming through or while still hot

**Recipe 36**

## Slow cooked Lamb & sweet potato curry

Prep 15 mins.
Cook 4-8 hours
Serves 4

- **Ingredients:**
- 
- 76g plain flour
- 1kg lamb, diced in large chunks (or Chicken)
- 500g sweet potato, peeled and cut into 2cm cubes
- 1 large brown onion, cut into thin wedges
- 400g can chickpeas, drained and rinsed
- 240g chicken stock
- 76g korma curry paste (Supermarket)
- 1 tbsp coriander, chopped
- 480g white rice, (serving suggestion)
- 

**Method:**

1. Combine flour, salt and pepper and coat the diced meat, then brown in a frying pan before adding to the slow cooker.

2. Add the vegetables, chickpeas and coriander.

3. Combine stock and curry paste and pour over the meat and vegetables in slow cooker.

4. Cover and cook on high for 4-5 hours or low for 8 hours.

Suggestion
Serve curry on a bed of white or saffron rice see rice in chapter Basic Cook

**Recipe 37**

## Slow cooker beef bourguignon

Prep 10 mins. Cook 8 hrs. Serves 4

- **Ingredients**
-
- 1 tbsp olive oil
- 600g casserole steak, cut into large chunks
- 1 large onion, peeled and chopped
- 6 rashers streaky bacon, roughly chopped
- 2 garlic cloves, peeled and chopped
- 325g carrots, peeled and chopped
- 300ml red wine
- 250ml beef stock
- 2 sprigs thyme
-
- **Method**
-
- Heat half the oil in a large frying pan. Season the meat and cook in the pan for 6-8 mins, until browned all over. Remove with a slotted spoon and put in a slow cooker.

- Add the remaining oil then the onion and bacon. Sauté for 4 mins before adding the garlic and carrots and cooking for a further 3-4 mins.
- Pour in the red wine and stir to help de-glaze the pan. Then stir in the stock.
- Pour the vegetables and liquid over the beef in the slow cooker.
- Add the sprigs of thyme and cook for 8 hrs on a low heat, until the beef is very tender. Serve with steamed cabbage and mashed potato.

**Recipe 38**

## Slow Roasted Lamb Shanks.........*Camp fire recipe*
*Given to me by a Dutch seasoned camper Margaret van Andel*

Serves 4, no time given for prep or cook.

### Ingredients

One lamb shank per person

1-2 litres of beef stock

1 bunch of rosemary

1 head of garlic (1 Bulb separate the cloves and crush)

1-2 potatoes per person

Packet of frozen veggies

Packet of gravy mix

Some plain flour

Small amount of oil

**Method**

Pre-heat camp oven on a good bed of coals.

Cut the meat away from the bone at the skinny end of the shank.

Cut small slits into shank to insert garlic and rosemary. Stuff a few bits of garlic and rosemary into the meat. Coat the meat with flour.

Place a small amount of oil into the camp oven that has been pre heated to bloody hot.

Brown off shanks in small amounts in the oven until sealed

Once all the shanks are nicely sealed remove the oven from the heat and deglaze the bottom with some of the red wine.

Then place the shanks in the oven and cover with the beef stock and red wine. Make sure you leave a glass of wine to drink

Then put the rest of the rosemary and garlic into the oven and put the lid on. Place the oven on the side of the fire and cover with coals.

Leave the oven for minimum 6hrs and drink rest of the wine.

**Potatoes**

Place one potato, a nob of butter, some finely diced garlic and some finely chopped rosemary into foil, one potato per person. Cover potatoes' tightly with foil and put into coals on fire. Cook until soft and brown.

**Veggies**

Steam or boil the vegies with the meat and potatoes are almost done.

**Gravy**

Once the shanks are done remove from oven and allow to rest.

Put the oven back onto the heat and reduce the remaining cooking juice and add some gravy mix.

Allow to thicken then strain to remove the garlic and rosemary.

Wisk to ensure gravy is smooth

.

Serving suggestion from Margaret.
Serve the potatoes and veggies on the side of the shank and cover with gravy and enjoy. Enjoy some more wine with dinner and a good yarn round the camp fire after you have had a great feed.

**Recipe 39**

# Smoky pork 'chilli'

**Slow cooker or sauce pan can recipe**

Prep 15 mins.
Cook 2 hrs in an oven, or 6-8 hours in a slow cooker.
Serves 4

### Ingredients

1 tbsp rapeseed oil

1 small onion, chopped

1 tsp caraway seeds

1 green pepper, seeded and chopped

1 clove garlic, thinly sliced

500g lean pork mince

½ tsp nutmeg

2 heaped tsp paprika

1 heaped tsp smoked paprika

1 x 400g tin chopped tomatoes

1 x 400g tin butterbeans

100g sweetcorn, fresh or frozen

Salt and freshly ground black pepper

## Method

Heat the oil in a large pan or casserole dish. Put in the onion and caraway seeds. Fry lightly for 5 minutes before adding the green pepper and garlic. Cook for a further 2 minutes.

Break up the mince with your hands and drop it into the pan. Sprinkle over the rest of the spices and season generously with salt and pepper. Turn the heat up and stir continuously until the meat is cooked through.

Add the tinned tomatoes and the butterbeans with half of their liquid. Bring up to simmering point and cook lid off for approximately 30 minutes. Meanwhile, preheat the oven to 160°C/140°C fan/Gas mark 3.

Transfer the chilli to an ovenproof dish if necessary and cover the dish with a lid or foil. Cook in the oven for a further 2 hours. Alternatively, transfer to a slow cooker and cook for 6–8 hours.

**Recipe 40**

## Spicy Couscous Fritters

Serves 4. Prep Time 20 mins. Cook time 40 minutes

- **Ingredients:**
-
- 250ml boiling water
- 125g couscous
- 1 long chilli, finely chopped, or 1 tsp chilli sauce
- 1 small handful flat leaf parsley
- 5 shallots, chopped
- 75g feta cheese
- 2 eggs
- 2 tbsp plain flour
- Olive oil
- Salt & pepper to taste
-

**Method:**

In a bowl place couscous and 250ml of boiling water.

Cover and stand for 15 minutes.

Allow to cool and then fluff with a fork.

Chop shallots, chilli and parsley.

Lightly beat the eggs.

When the couscous is cold, add all ingredients, except the oil, in a bowl and mix together with hands. Crumble the feta.

Make patties about the size of a doughnut

To cook, place oil in non-stick frying pan.

Cook until golden brown.

Suggestion Serve with plain yoghurt or a side salad or roast vegetables.

**Recipe 41**

## Spring chicken stew with tarragon butter

Prep 10 mins

Cook 1 hr 10 mins.

Serves 6

### Ingredients

1.5kg whole chicken

30g pack fresh tarragon

30g butter, softened

8 shallots, trimmed and peeled

250g new potatoes, halved if large

200g pack baby carrots

12 radishes, 8 trimmed and halved, 4 thinly sliced to serve

450ml fresh chicken stock, or made using ½ a chicken stock cube

250g broad beans, defrosted if frozen, skinned

**Method**

Start by **jointing** the chicken. Place the chicken, breast-side up, on a board. Use a sharp knife to make a cut between the breast and the leg on each side of the bird, following the curve of the body to remove the legs and thighs, including the fleshy oysters on the back. Cut through the middle joint of each leg to separate the thigh and drumstick, and again between the drumstick and the knuckle at the end (discard the knuckles or freeze, with the backbone from step 2, for stock).

To remove the breast and wings, cut down one side of the breastbone, going right through the bone into the cavity. Repeat on the other side. With poultry shears or sharp kitchen scissors, cut each breast away from the backbone. Separate the wing and breast joint by cutting each breast joint in half about 2cm from the wing.

Season the chicken pieces. Strip the leaves from two-thirds of the tarragon sprigs and finely chop, discarding the stalks. In a bowl, mash half the chopped tarragon into the butter with a fork. Carefully loosen the skin on the chicken pieces and rub the butter between the meat and skin.

Heat a large flameproof casserole dish over a medium-high heat. Add the chicken, skin-side down, and fry for 5 mins, turning halfway, until golden. Add the shallots and fry for 5 mins

Add the potatoes, carrots, halved radishes and the stock to the dish. Bring to the boil, then reduce the heat, cover and simmer for 55 mins. Add the broad beans, cover and cook for 5 mins more or until the vegetables and chicken are cooked through, with no pink meat showing.

Stir the reserved chopped tarragon into the pan juices. Just before serving, scatter over the sliced radishes and remaining tarragon sprigs, and season with black pepper.

**Tip:** Jointing a chicken ... refer to the chapter in Basic cook at the back of this book
Don't fancy jointing a chicken? Use a 1kg pack of chicken thighs instead.

**Recipe 42**

## Sweet Onion Chicken

Prep 20 mins. Cook 20 mins. Serves 2

### Ingredients
- 2 tsp sunflower oil
- 1 medium onion, peeled and finely chopped
- 2 bird's eye (Thai) chillies, finely chopped
- 3 garlic cloves, peeled and grated
- 2.5cm (1in) piece fresh root ginger, peeled and grated
- A pinch of salt
- 1 tomato, diced
- 2 × 150g skinless, boneless chicken breasts, cut into cubes
- ½ tsp ground cumin
- 1 tsp coarsely ground black pepper

- 1 small handful of fresh coriander, chopped
-

## Method

Heat the oil in a wide frying pan over a medium-high heat. When hot, add the onion, chillies, garlic, ginger and salt. Stir-fry for 2 mins before reducing the heat and cooking gently for a further 5 min.

Increase the heat to medium, put in the tomato and stir-fry for 2 mins. Add the chicken, cumin and pepper and stir-fry for a further 5 minutes.

Reduce the heat to low, pour in 150ml water, stir and cook for another 5 minutes. If there seems to be too much liquid, increase the heat and boil for 1–2 minutes.

Stir in the coriander before serving.

**Recipe 43**

## Garlic chicken

Prep 15 mins. Cook 35 mins. Serves 4

### Ingredients

4 chicken breast fillets
1 tsp salt
¾ tsp ground black pepper
2 tablespoons olive oil
1 onion, thinly sliced
2 bulbs garlic (crush the cloves)
1 (400g) tin chopped tomatoes
1 tbsp dried basil
1 tsp of dried oregano
1 tbsp dried rosemary

## Method

Season the chicken with the salt and pepper.

Preheat frying pan over a medium to high putting 2 tbsp olive oil in.

Add the chicken, onion and crushed garlic cloves and cook until the chicken is a deep golden brown, approx. 4-6 minutes each side.

Reduce heat to medium and cook for a further 6-8 minutes or when pricked by a fork the chicken juices run clear.

Pour the tinned tomatoes over the chicken, sprinkle over the herbs and stir into the sauce, then simmer for about 15 mins before serving.

**Recipe 44**

## Teriyaki Salmon one pot

Prep 15 mins. Cook 20-25 mins. Serves 1

### Ingredients

Non-stick foil, 12x18 inches
25g carrots, thinly sliced
175g broccoli florets, sliced
Olive oil to taste
Salt & pepper to taste
175g skinless salmon
2 tbsp teriyaki sauce (local supermarket)

### Method

Preheat oven to 190°C/Gas Mark 5

Fold the foil in half, then open.

On one half, lay down the broccoli and carrots. Drizzle on the oil and sprinkle on salt & pepper.

Lay the salmon on the veggies and pour on the teriyaki sauce. (If the Salmon is frozen allow a minimum of two hours to defrost before using)

Fold the foil over the salmon and close together by folding it over itself along the edges.

Bake for 20-25 minutes

Serve

**Recipe 45**

## Tomato Pesto Salmon One Pot

Prep 15 mins. Cook 30-35 mins.

Serves 1

### Ingredients

Non-stick foil, 12x18 inches

75g green beans sliced length ways

Olive oil to taste

Salt & pepper to taste

175g skinless salmon

2 tbsp pesto

8 cherry tomatoes, halved

### Method

Preheat oven to 180°C/Gas Mark 5

Fold the foil in half, then open.

On one half, lay down the green beans. Drizzle on oil and sprinkle on salt and pepper.

Lay the salmon on the green beans and spread on the pesto. Top with tomatoes. (If the Salmon is frozen allow a minimum of two hours to defrost before using.)

Fold the foil over the salmon and close the foil together by folding it over itself along the edges.

Bake for 20-25 minutes, then serve

**Recipe 46**

## Traditional Goulash

Prep 30 mins.

Cook in the oven for 3 hours or in a slow cooker on low for 8 hours or overnight

Serves 4

### Ingredients

400g extra lean casserole beef steak, diced

1 tbsp plain flour

Salt and ground black pepper

2 tbsp sunflower oil

1 large onion, chopped

2 garlic cloves, peeled and chopped

1 green pepper, deseeded and chopped

1 red pepper, deseeded and chopped

1 heaped tbsp paprika

1 heaped tsp smoked paprika

1 × 400g can chopped tomatoes

250ml beef stock (fresh or made with 1 cube)

150ml light crème fraiche

## Method

Sprinkle the beef with the flour and salt and pepper and toss until well coated.
Heat the oil in a casserole dish over a high heat. Brown the steak in batches and set aside.

Turn the heat to low and add the onion, garlic and peppers. Put the lid on and sweat until tender, about 10 minutes.

Return the beef to the pan together with both types of paprika, the chopped tomatoes and beef stock. Bring to a simmer and cook with the lid off for 20–30 minutes.
On the hob: Continue to cook over a low heat for about 1 hour, removing the lid towards the end of the cooking time.

 In the oven: Preheat the oven to 150C/130C fan/Gas Mark 2 and cook for 3 hours.
In the slow cooker: Transfer to a slow cooker and cook on low for 8 hours or overnight.
Stir in the crème fraiche just before serving.

The goulash freezes well, and this can be done before the crème fraiche is added.

**Recipe 47**

## Vegetable pockets

- **Required**
- Tin Foil
- Bar-B-Q or camp fire
- Prep 15 mins. Cook 20-30 mins
- Serves 4
- 
- **Ingredients**
- Butter as required
- Garlic (fresh or dry)
- 2 diced carrots
- 1 diced onion
- 2 diced potatoes or medium diced sweet potatoes
- 3 diced chicken breasts or 6 sausages
- 4 corn on the cob

- 
- **Method**
- Cut and dice all the vegetables except the corn. Add a teaspoon of butter, seasoning and garlic.
- Place on a square piece of foil with either diced raw chicken or a sausage.
- Gather up the foil and make into 4 pockets.
- Season and brush the corn on the cob with butter and wrap in foil.
- Cook on a fire where the coals that have died down a bit, or BBQ.
- Cook until veggies are softened which is about 15-20 mins, depending on the fire coals or BBQ.
  Serve and enjoy.

**Recipe 48**

## Vegetable Crumble

SERVES 4

Prep 20 mins.

Ready in 1hr 30 mins

Serves 4

## Ingredients

2 tbsp olive oil

1 large onion, peeled and chopped

2 garlic cloves, peeled and sliced

1 red chilli, deseeded and chopped

1×400g can chopped tomatoes

300ml white wine

500ml vegetable stock (2 vegetable cubes)

1 bay leaf 2 fresh thyme sprigs (or ½ tsp dried)

600g butternut squash (about 1 large), peeled, de-seeded and cut into chunks

1×400g can butterbeans, rinsed and drained

50g wholemeal breadcrumbs

5g (1 tsp) Parmesan, grated

25g chopped nuts

handful of fresh parsley, chopped

Salt and freshly ground black pepper


## Method


Heat 1 tablespoon of oil in a large pan, add the onion and fry gently for 8 minutes. Add the garlic and chilli and fry for a further 2 minutes.

Stir in the chopped tomatoes, white wine, vegetable stock, bay leaf and thyme. Bring to the boil, then reduce the heat to medium–low and simmer, uncovered, for 20 minutes.

Add the butternut squash and cook for a further 20 minutes. Stir in the butter beans.

Preheat the oven 180C/160C fan/Gas Mark 5

Mix the breadcrumbs, parmesan, chopped nuts, parsley and the remaining tablespoon of oil together.

Transfer the vegetable sauce to a suitable casserole dish and sprinkle on the crumble topping. Season liberally with salt and pepper. Bake in the oven for 30 minutes or until the crumble is golden and crisp.

## Biscuits & Dessert Index

1. Apple Crumble

2. Bread & Butter Pudding

3. Breakfast Banana Bread

4. Butter Biscuits

5. Carrot Cake Biscuits

6. Chocolate Chip Biscuits

7. Chocolate & Banana Biscuits

8. Chocolate & Vanilla Biscuits

9. Gingerbread Men

10. Jam Drop Biscuits

11. Peanut Butter Biscuits

12. Raspberry Trifle

13. Shortbread Biscuits

14. Smarty Biscuits

15. Strawberry Cake

16.Strawberry Roll Dessert

17. Sweet Oat Biscuits

**Recipe 1**

## Apple Crumble

or if you replace the apple with Rhubarb, or Blackberry's or Pear they all make a good crumble

Prep 10 mins. Cook 30-40 mins. Serves 4

- **Ingredients**
- 
- 650g Bramley cooking apples, peeled, cored and diced into small chunks
- 2 tbsp caster sugar (28g)
- 1 tsp vanilla
- 110g self-raising flour
- 40g demerara sugar, plus 1 tbsp for sprinkling
- 40g cold salted butter, diced
- 2 tbsp oatmeal (12g)
- custard, cream or ice cream to serve

## Method

Heat oven to 200°C/ fan 180°C/Gas Mark 6. Place the Bramley apples, caster sugar, vanilla and 1½ tbsp of water in a saucepan and gently cook for a few minutes until the apples have softened. Taste and add a little more sugar if needed, depending on how tart the apples are. Transfer to a greased ovenproof dish.

Put the flour, demerara sugar and butter into a mixing bowl and rub with your fingertips until it resembles breadcrumbs, then stir in the oatmeal. Scatter onto the apples and then sprinkle the extra sugar on top. Bake for about 30-40 minutes until golden and bubbling. Serve with custard, cream or ice cream.

Reci pe 2

## Bread and Butter Pudding

Prep 20 mins. Cook 35-40 mins. Serves 6

### Ingredients

- 60g lightly salted butter, softened
- 10 slices thinly sliced white bread, preferably a day old
- 60g sultanas
- 1/2 lemon, finely grated, zest only
- 350ml whole milk
- 100ml double cream
- 3 eggs
- 60g golden caster sugar
- 1 tsp vanilla extract
- grated fresh nutmeg
- 
- **Method**
- Preheat the oven to 180°C/fan 160°C/Gas Mark 4. Lightly butter a medium sized baking dish (approximately 20cm x 25cm) with 10g of the butter. Spread the remaining butter generously over one side of the bread slices. Cut each slice into quarters.
- Arrange half the bread quarters, buttered sides up, over the base of the buttered dish and scatter with half the sultanas and lemon zest. Repeat to use up all the buttered bread, sultanas and lemon zest.

- Heat the milk and cream together in a small saucepan until steaming hot. Meanwhile, whisk the eggs with 50g of the golden caster sugar, until pale and thick. Slowly pour the hot milk mixture onto the eggs, whisking constantly. Strain through a sieve into a jug, then stir in the vanilla extract.
- Slowly pour the custard over the bread pudding, being careful to soak all the bread. Scatter the surface with the remaining sugar and grate over a little nutmeg. Bake for 35-40 minutes in the centre of the oven, until golden brown. Let the pudding rest for 5-10 minutes before serving.

**Recipe 3**

## Breakfast Banana Bread

Prep 15mins.

Cook 1 hr 10 mins.
Serves 10

### Ingredients

2 medium eggs

200g Demerara sugar

100g butter, melted and cooled

3 large ripe bananas

75g full fat Greek yogurt

1tsp vanilla extract

200g plain flour

1tsp baking powder

110g blueberries

25g (1oz) chopped hazelnuts

Greek yogurt, to serve or honey, to serve

**Method**

Preheat the oven to 190°C/fan 170°C/Gas Mark 5. Grease and line a 2lb (900g) loaf tin with non-stick baking paper. With an electric whisk, mix the eggs, sugar, cooled butter and a good pinch of salt together for 4 minutes until light and fluffy. Mash the banana and yogurt with a fork, add to the eggs with the vanilla extract and whisk again.

Add a spoonful of the flour to the blueberries and mix to coat. Stir the baking powder into the remaining flour and sift this over the top of the whisked eggs and banana. Fold through, then add the blueberries and fold again until everything is just combined. Spoon into your prepared tin, even out the top and sprinkle over the hazelnuts. Bake in the oven for 1 hour 10 minutes, until a skewer comes away clean. Cool in the tin for 15 minutes, then turn out and cool completely on a wire rack. Serve with Greek yogurt and a drizzle of clear honey.

**Freezing and defrosting guidelines**

Bake according to the recipe but stop before adding decoration. Allow to cool completely. Wrap well in clingfilm and tin foil (to prevent freezer burn) and freeze for up to 3 months.

Loosen the tin foil and clingfilm but leave to defrost in packaging at room temperature for several hours before serving.

If you wish to add icing or decoration, add them after the baked loaf has fully defrosted and is at room temperature.

**Recipe 4**

**Butter Biscuits**

Prep 15 Mins.

Cook 45 Mins.

Makes 30
**Ingredients**

250 g butter softened

177g caster sugar

1/2 tsp vanilla essence

225 self-raising flour

**Method**

Using your hands knead all the ingredients together well.

Roll into small walnut-sized balls and put onto sprayed biscuit trays.

Flatten with a fork or back of a spoon.

Decorate with slivers of almond or pecans or halved glazed cherries.

Bake at 170-180C/Gas Mark 4 for about 15-20 minutes.

**Recipe 5**

## Carrot Cake Biscuits

Prep 15 mins.
Cook 15 mins.
Makes 25

- **Ingredients**
- 125 g unsalted butter
- 175g light brown sugar
- 125 g plain flour
- 125 g wholemeal plain flour
- 1 tsp baking powder
- 1 tsp ground cinnamon
- 1/2 tsp nutmeg
- 1/4 tsp ground cardamom
- 50 g carrots coarsely grated
- 150 g sultanas

**Method**

Preheat oven to 200C/Gas Mark 6. Line a couple of baking trays with non-stick foil. Beat together butter, sugar and honey until light and fluffy. Add eggs one at a time, beating well between each addition. Add flours, baking powder and spices and stir to combine, then fold through the grated carrots and sultanas

Form into dessertspoon-size balls and place on the baking trays, pressing down slightly on top. Bake for 12-15 minutes until golden and cooked through.

**Recipe 6**

## Chocolate Chip Biscuits

Prep 15 mins.
Cook 15 mins.
Makes 20 or possibly more

**Ingredients**

180 g butter softened
75 g caster sugar
125 ml sweetened condensed milk
225g self-raising flour
250 g dark chocolate bits

**Method**

Preheat oven to 180C/Gas Mark 4. Using an electric mixer, beat the butter and sugar together until light and creamy, then beat in the condensed milk.

Add the flour and mix on low speed until smooth. Stir in the chocolate bits until well combined.

Roll about 2 teaspoonfuls of the mixture into balls and place on the foil lined trays. Press each ball with a floured fork.

Bake for 12 - 15 minutes or until lightly golden. Remove from oven and allow to cool on the trays. Store in airtight containers.

**Note**

I have also made these using white or milk chocolate bits.

**Recipe 7**

## Chocolate-Banana Biscuits

Prep 15 mins. Cook 20-30 mins. Makes 28

**Ingredients**

125 g butter
115g caster sugar
65g brown sugar firmly packed
1 egg
245 g self-raising flour sifted
75 g banana mashed
75 g dark chocolate bits

**Method**

Lightly grease two oven trays. Beat the butter and both sugars together in a small bowl with an electric mixer until the mixture is light and fluffy. Add the egg and beat until well combined. Stir in the sifted flour, bananas and choc-bits.

Drop level tablespoons of mixture, about 3 cm apart, on the prepared oven trays. Cook at 180C/Gas Mark 4 for about 20 minutes, or until the cookies are lightly browned. Cool on trays.

**Recipe 8**

## Chocolate and Vanilla Biscuits

Prep 15 mins. Cook Time 00:20

Cook 20 mins.

Makes 16

### Ingredients

240 g plain flour
175g caster sugar
200 g butter brought to room temperature
1 egg
1 tsp vanilla bean paste
1 1/2 tbs cocoa powder

- **Method**
-

- Using a food processor, process flour and sugar until combined. Add butter and process until mixture resembles a breadcrumb texture. Add egg, vanilla bean paste and 1 tablespoon iced water and process until dough comes together as a ball.

- Divide the dough in half. Set aside one half and to the other half add cocoa powder and process until combined.

- Press each dough half into a 20cm circle between two sheets of baking paper. Chill in the fridge for 20 minutes

- Preheat oven to 180C/Gas Mark 4. Line 3 large baking trays with baking paper.

- With a rolling pin, roll out each dough half to 4-5mm thick. Using an **8cm x 10.5cm biscuit cutter**, cut out 8 rounds from each dough, re-rolling scraps as you go. Place the biscuits on 2 prepared trays as you go. Chill for 10 minutes

- With **a 5cm x 6.5cm biscuit cutter**, cut out chocolate and vanilla round from the round biscuits and place on third tray as you go. Chill trays again if dough is getting to soft to handle.

- Place chocolate hearts inside vanilla biscuits and vanilla hearts inside chocolate biscuits.

- Bake for 17-18 minutes or until light golden. Cool on trays.

- **Notes**

- You could add some pink colouring to the vanilla batch of dough for pink and chocolate biscuits or skip the cocoa and have a batch of vanilla and pink biscuits.

- Store cooled biscuits in an airtight container for up to 1 week.

**Recipe 9**

## Gingerbread Men

Prep 30mins. Cook 15 mins.  Makes 40

- **Ingredients**
- 
- 360g plain flour
- 120g butter chopped
- 2 tsp bicarbonate of soda
- 1/2 tsp ground cloves
- 2 tsp ground ginger
- 65g brown sugar
- 170gg golden syrup
- 1 egg

- 2 tsp ground cinnamon

**Method**

Preheat oven to 160C/Gas Mark 3.
 Combine all the ingredients in a large bowl and knead until smooth.
Roll between 2 sheets of baking paper until approximately 2.5 cm thick.
Refrigerate until chilled.
Place chilled dough on a board and cut out shapes.
Place on baking paper-lined tray.
Bake for 10-15 minutes until lightly golden.

**Recipe 10**

## Jam Drops Biscuits

Prep 5 mins.
Cook 15 mins.
Makes 20

## Ingredients

2 eggs
35 g sugar
250 g self-raising flour
125 g butter
165 g strawberry jam

**Method**

Cream butter and sugar. Add eggs one at a time and beat in.
Add flour and mix into a stiff dough.

Break dough into small pieces, press hole in centre with a cork, or similar and fill with jam.
Bake at 180C/Gas Mark 4 for about 15 minutes.
Note; Made using just 5 ingredients!

**Recipe 11**

## Peanut Butter Biscuits

Prep 10 mins. Cook 15 mins.  Makes 24

### Ingredients

110 g brown sugar
115 g caster sugar
115 g butter melted
125 g peanut butter
1 egg
245 g self-raising flour
1 tsp vanilla essence

### Method

Combine the sugars, then add the melted butter and lightly beaten egg. Mix well.
Gradually add the sifted flour and remaining ingredients, mixing thoroughly.
Place teaspoonfuls of mixture onto a greased tray, flattening with a fork.
Bake for about 12-15 minutes at 160C/Gas Mark 3.
**Notes** Use a generous measure of peanut butter.

**Recipe 12**

## Raspberry Trifle

Serves 6    Prep 25-30 mins.

- **Ingredients**
- 450 g Betty Crocker Red Velvet Cake Mix cooked
- 85g raspberry jelly
- 750g custard
- 300 ml whipped cream
- 440g sliced tinned peaches (drain and reserve juice)
- fresh raspberries *to decorate
- 1 tbsp milk chocolate grated *to decorate optional
- 2 tbsp pistachios chopped *to decorate optional
- 1 tbsp sherry (optional) **Method**
- Make the cake to the packet instructions preferably using a square tin. Allow to cool completely.
- Allow jelly to set until almost fully set. If it sets too firm, remove from the fridge for approximately ½ hour before assembling the trifle.
- 
- **Assembly:**
- Slice cake into 2cm wide slices.

- Line a 2.5 litre capacity glass bowl with the cake slices. If the cake is dry, sprinkle with some peach juice or sherry.
- Roughly chop/break up the jelly and distribute across the surface of the cake and up the sides of the bowl.
- Arrange the peach slices over the jelly then cover with custard.
- Top with the whipped cream.
- Garnish with fresh berries, chopped pistachios and grated chocolate.
- Refrigerate until required.

Recipe 13

## Shortbread Biscuits

Prep 15 mins.   Cook 35 mins.  Makes 40
**Ingredients**

- 250 g butter softened
- 10 g butter
- 190 g caster sugar
- 325 g plain flour
- 35 g rice flour
- 200 g salted caramel dessert sauce
- 125 g dark chocolate chopped
- 
- **Method**
- Using an electric mixer with a paddle attachment, beat the butter and sugar until light and fluffy, add the flours and beat until the dough comes together, or use your hands.
- Turn onto a lightly floured surface and knead until smooth. Divide into 2 batches.
- Roll each batch between 2 sheets of baking paper until 5mm thick. Chill for 30 minutes.

- Preheat oven to 150C/Gas Mark 2. Line 2 large baking tray with baking paper.
- Using a **5cm cutter**, cut out rounds. Place on prepared trays. Reroll scraps to make about 40 biscuits. Bake for 30-35 minutes or until light golden. Cool on trays.
- Spread with caramel.
- Place chocolate in a microwave safe bowl. Microwave on high (100%) for 1 minute. Stir, then microwave in 30 second bursts stirring each time, until smooth. Add extra butter and stir to combine.
- Spread the chocolate mixture over the caramel and stand for 1 hour to set.

**Recipe 14**

## Smarty Biscuits

Prep 30 mins.    Cook 15 mins.
Makes 35

- **Ingredients**
- 
- 100 g butter melted
- 115g caster sugar
- 1 tsp vanilla essence
- 1 egg lightly beaten
- 210g self-raising flour
- 2 tubes of smarties
- 

**Method**

Preheat oven to 180C/Gas Mark 4.
Line your baking trays with baking paper.
Combine the butter, sugar, vanilla and egg in a bowl.

Add the flour and stir until combined.

Cover and refrigerate for 15 minutes until firm. 6 Roll teaspoons of mixture into small balls. Place on tray and press down slightly.

Top with Smarties, sprinkles, or chocolate chips.

Bake for 15 minutes until golden.

Stand for 5 minutes then transfer to a wire rack to cool.

**Notes**

You can also make jam drops with this recipe. Just make an indent with the end of a wooden spoon and add a dollop of jam before baking.

**Recipe 15**

## Strawberry Cake

Prep 30 mins.   Cook 20 mins. Makes 15

- **Ingredients**
- 150 g dried strawberries
- 250g self-raising flour
- 115g sugar
- 100g desiccated coconut
- 185 g butter melted
- **For Icing**
- 170g sifted icing sugar,
- 2 tablespoons lemon juice
- 
- **Method**
- 
- Soak strawberries in hot water for 30 minutes and then drain.

- Add all ingredients and mix well.
- Press into a cake tin and bake at 190C/Gas Mark 5 for 20 minutes.
- Once cool, ice with pink icing if desired.
- **Notes.**
- If you can't find dried strawberries, use fresh.
- To make the pink icing, use 1 1/2 cups sifted icing sugar, 2 tablespoons lemon juice and pink food colouring.
- Place the icing sugar and lemon juice in a bowl and mix well until smooth. Add a drop of the colouring and mix to combine.
- Pour over cooled cake and place in the fridge for 30 minutes to set. Slice and serve.

**Recipe 16**

## Strawberry Roll Dessert

Prep 15 mins.    Cook 30 mins. Serves 8

- **Ingredients**
  - 4 egg whites
  - 35g sugar
  - 1 tsp white vinegar
  - 1 tsp cornflour
  - 1 tsp vanilla essence
  - 300 ml whipped cream
  - 250 g fresh strawberries
  - 2 passionfruit optional
  - 
- **Method**
- Grease a swiss roll tin and line with baking paper. Preheat oven to 180C/Gas Mark 4.

- Beat the egg whites until soft peaks form.
- Add sugar gradually and continue beating until mixture is stiff and glossy and all sugar is dissolved.
- Gently fold through the vanilla, cornflour and vinegar.
- Spread the meringue evenly into a prepared tin. Bake for 25-30 minutes.
- Allow to cool completely before turning out onto sugared baking paper.
- Spread with whipped cream and top with sliced strawberries.
- Roll up from long side and place on serving plate, still covered with the baking paper.
- Refrigerate for 24 hours.
- Decorate the top with strawberries and passionfruit if desired.

**Recipe 17**

## Sweet Oat Biscuits

Prep 10 mins.    Cook 15-20mins.

### Ingredients

125g plain flour
140g rolled oats
195g brown sugar
50g coconut
125 g butter
2 tbs golden syrup
1 tbs water
1/2 tsp bicarbonate of soda

### Method

Sift the flour into a bowl. Add the sugar, rolled oats and coconut.

Melt the butter in a saucepan, then add golden syrup and water.
Stir the bicarbonate of soda into the liquid mixture.
Add the liquid to the dry ingredients and mix thoroughly.
Place walnut-sized balls of mixture on a greased tray and bake at 190C/Gas Mark 4 for 15-20 minutes.
Biscuits will harden when cool.

# BBQ Index

1. BBQ Chicken Kebabs with Garlic & Lemon

2. BBQ Chicken Wings

3. BBQ Gammon Steaks

4. BBQ Salmon Sandwich

5. BBQ Salmon with a Twist

6. BBQ Salmon with Chilli & Garlic

7. BBQ Tandoori Chicken/Turkey Naan

8. Chicken Honey/Soy Kebabs

9. Chicken Tortillas

10. Courgette & Feta Patties

11. Cumberland Hot Dogs with Tomato Salsa

12. Grilled Corn on the Cob with Chilli & Lime

13. Lamb Kebabs

14. Marinated Turkey Kebabs

15. Mini One Pot Dinner in Foil

16. Mr. Posh's BBQ Salmon

17. Pineapple Soy Chicken Skewers

18. Porcini Rubber Steak

19. Pork & Thyme Cheeseburgers

20. Potato Salad with Broad Beans

21. Seared Steak with Chimichurri Dressing

22. Teriyaki BBQ Shrimp Skewered

**Recipe 1**

# BBQ Chicken Kebabs with Garlic & lemon

Serves 2.    Prep 10mins.

Cook 15 mins.


**Ingredients**


4 chicken breasts

60g (2 oz) butter

4 garlic cloves crushed

grated rind and juice of 1 lemon

1 tbsp of brown sugar

**Method**

Cut chicken into small pieces.

Melt the butter then add garlic, lemon juice, grated lemon rind, and brown sugar.

Add the chicken to the mixture and marinate for at least 1 hour.

Put the chicken onto skewers then baste with the remaining mixture while turning.

**Recipe 2**

## BBQ Chicken Wings

Serves 2    Prep 10 mins.

Cook 20-25 mins.

**Ingredients**

8 chicken wings

1 tsp paprika

1 tsp Salt

1 tbsp flour

1 tbsp mixed herbs

Plastic bag

**Method**

Combine damp chicken wings into a plastic bag with the paprika, salt, flour & mixed herbs

Shake until all the wings are coated with the mix.

Heat your grill with cover over on a high heat for 10 minutes, then turn the grill to medium heat. Cook the wings with cover until the colour is a light brown and the skin has rendered some fat. Flip once during cooking.

Transfer to a serving plate immediately.

Serve with side salad, cherry tomatoes and crusty French rolls.

**Recipe 3**

## BBQ Gammon Steaks

Serves 4.   Prep 10 mins.

Cook 15 mins.

**Ingredients**

220g dark brown soft sugar

4 tbsp lemon juice

5 tbsp horseradish

2 slices gammon

**Method**

Preheat a barbecue to high heat and lightly oil the cooking grate.

In a small bowl, mix the sugar, lemon juice and horseradish.

Heat the sugar mixture in the microwave on high heat for a minute or until warm. Alternatively, heat the mixture in a pan on the grill stirring continuously until the sugar has melted.

Score both sides of gammon. Place on the prepared barbecue. Baste continuously with the dark brown soft sugar mixture while cooking.

Grill for 6 to 8 minutes per side or to desired taste.

**Recipe 4**

## BBQ salmon sandwich

Serves 2.   Prep 15 mins. Cook 8 mins.

- **Ingredients**
- 4 rashers streaky bacon
- 1 (450g) fillet salmon, cut into 2 portions
- 1 tbsp olive oil
- 5 tbsp mayonnaise
- 1 tsp dried dill
- 1 tsp freshly grated lemon zest
- 4 slices good crusty bread, toasted
- 4 slices tomatoes, halved
- 2 lettuce leaves, shredded
- 
- **Method**

- Cook the bacon in a large, deep frying pan over medium-high heat until evenly browned, then drain on kitchen paper.
- Preheat an outdoor barbecue to medium-high heat and lightly oil the grate.
- Evenly coat the salmon with the olive oil, then cook on the preheated barbecue with the skin side down for about 5 minutes before turning and cooking on the other side until the skin can easily be lifted off the flesh, about 5 minutes more. Turn the salmon once more and continue cooking until the salmon flakes easily with a fork.
- Whisk the mayonnaise, dill and lemon zest together in a small bowl; divide between 2 of the toasted bread slices. Top each with a portion of cooked salmon, 2 tomato slices, 2 bacon slices, 1 lettuce leaf and the remaining slice of toasted bread.

**Recipe 5**


## BBQ Salmon with a twist


Serves 16.   Prep 10 mins.

Cook 15-20 mins.

**Ingredients**

200g dark brown soft sugar

175g honey

1 dash Worcester sauce

125ml cider vinegar

1 (2kg) whole salmon/trout fillet

**Method**

Preheat the barbecue to high heat.

In a small bowl, mix together the sugar, honey, Worcester sauce and vinegar.

Brush one side of the salmon with the basting sauce the put it on the barbecue basted side down. After about 7 minutes, generously baste the top, then turn the salmon over. Cook for about 8 more minutes, then brush on more basting sauce, turn and cook for 2 minutes.

Take care not to overcook the salmon as it will lose its juices and flavour if cooked too long.

Serve with salad.

**Recipe 6**

## BBQ Salmon with Chilli and Garlic

Serves 6.   Prep 15 mins.
Cook 30 mins.

- **Ingredients**
- 1 (1.3kg) whole salmon, cleaned
- 4 tbsp soy sauce
- 1 tbsp chilli sauce
- 1 tbsp chopped fresh root ginger
- 1 clove garlic, chopped
- 1tbsp dark brown soft sugar
- 3 spring onions, chopped
- juice and zest of 1 lime
- 
**Method**

Preheat the barbecue to high heat.

Trim the tail and fins off the salmon. Make several shallow cuts across the salmon's skin, then place the salmon on a large sheet of aluminium foil.

In a bowl, stir together soy sauce, chilli sauce, ginger and garlic. Mix in lime juice, lime zest and the sugar. Spoon the sauce over the salmon.

Fold the foil over the salmon and crimp the edges to seal. (making an envelope)

If using hot charcoals, move them to one side of the barbecue. Place the fish on the side of the barbecue that does not have coals directly underneath it and close the lid. If using a gas barbecue, place the fish on one side, and turn off the flames directly underneath it and close the lid. Cook for 25 to 30 minutes. Remove to a serving platter and pour any juices that may have collected in the foil over the top of the fish. Sprinkle with spring onions.

**Recipe 7**

## BBQ Tandoori Chicken/ Turkey Naan

Serves 4.  Prep 10 mins.
Cook 5-10 mins.

- **Ingredients**
- 500g chicken/turkey mince
- 25g fresh breadcrumbs
- 1 tsp tandoori paste
- 1 tsp olive oil
- 125 mls reduced-fat plain yoghurt
- shredded cucumber (squeeze and drain excess water)
- lettuce (any variety), leaves separated, washed, shredded
- Salt and pepper
- Naan bread
-

**Method**

- Mix chicken mince, breadcrumbs and tandoori paste in a bowl.
- Divide the mixture into even portions and shape each portion into burger sized patties.
- Heat oil on the BBQ and cook the patties for approximately 4 minutes each side or until golden brown.
- Meanwhile, mix yogurt and cucumber in a bowl and season with salt and pepper.
- Warm the Naan bread on the BBQ.
- To serve, place the lettuce, patties and cucumber yogurt mix on top of Naan bread and roll into cone shaped wrap.

**Recipe 8**

## Chicken Honey/Soy Kebabs

Serves 12.    Prep 15 mins. Cook 15 mins.

**Ingredients**

4 tbsp vegetable oil
5 tbsp honey
5 tbsp soy sauce
1/4 tsp freshly ground black pepper
8 skinless, boneless chicken breast fillets - cut into cubes
2 cloves garlic
5 onions, cut into pieces
2 red peppers, cut into pieces

**Method**

In a large bowl, whisk together oil, honey, soy sauce and pepper. Before adding the chicken, reserve a small amount of marinade to brush onto the kebabs while cooking. Place the chicken, garlic, onions and peppers in the bowl, and marinate in the refrigerator at least 2 hours (the longer the better).

Preheat barbecue to high heat.

Drain the marinade from the chicken and vegetables, and discard. Thread the chicken and vegetables alternately onto the skewers. (If using wooden skewers soak in cold water for about 30 minutes so they won't burn)

Lightly oil the cooking grate. Cook the kebabs for 12-15 minutes, or until the chicken juices run clear and the chicken is cooked through. Turn and brush with reserved marinade frequently.

**Recipe 9**

## Chicken tortillas

Serves 4.   Prep 10 mins. Cook 15 mins.

- **Ingredients**
- 1 tbsp extra virgin olive oil
- 1 tsp cumin powder
- 1 tsp chilli powder
- ½ tsp dried oregano
- 3 crushed garlic cloves
- Juice of 1 lime
- Pinch salt & black pepper
- 500g chicken breast cut into cubes
- 1 red pepper cut into 4cm squares
- 1 yellow pepper cut into 4cm squares
- 1 red onion cut in wedges 2 layers thick

- 4 flour tortillas
- Olive oil spray

## Method

Combine the olive oil, cumin, chilli powder, oregano, garlic, lime juice, salt and pepper. Use this to marinade the chicken and vegetables separately in sealable plastic bags.

Chill in a fridge if available for 2 hours or use straight away.

BBQ/campfire. Thread chicken, pepper and onions onto skewers, alternating as you go.

Grill/flame skewers, turning them frequently, for 5 to 8 minutes.

Wrap tortillas in foil and place on grill to warm.

Serve with tortillas and desired toppings.

**Recipe 10**

## Courgette & Feta Patties

Serves 4.   Prep 15 mins.

Cook 15 mins.

**Ingredients**:

2 courgettes grated

2 medium carrots grated

2 spring onions, finely chopped

50g parmesan cheese, grated

2 eggs, beaten

200g feta, crumbled

200g flour

Oil to fry

**Method:**

Mix all ingredients together in a bowl.

Combine and cover for 30 minutes in a fridge to firm up.

Shape into patties.

Cook on an oiled BBQ or in a frying pan until golden

Serve with a salad

**Recipe 11**

## Cumberland Hot Dogs with Tomato Salsa

Serves 4.   Prep 10 mins.

Cook 15 mins.

**Ingredients**

4 Cumberland sausages

4 tomatoes, halved

1 red chilli, finely chopped

1 garlic clove, finely chopped

2 tbsp chopped basil

pinch brown sugar

2 tbsp olive oil

1 tbsp red wine vinegar

hot dog rolls, salad leaves and soured cream, to serve

**Method**

Barbecue the sausages for 10-15 mins, turning occasionally, until cooked through.

Meanwhile cook the tomatoes, cut side up, for 3-4 mins, until the skins start to blacken. Transfer to a bowl.

Mash the tomatoes with a fork and stir in the remaining ingredients. Spoon some into a long roll, add salad leaves, a sausage and top with a splash of soured cream.

**Recipe 12**

# Lamb kebabs

Serves 2.   Prep 15 mins.

Cook 15 mins.

**Ingredients**

1 lamb neck fillet, cut into cubes

3 peppers (red, green and yellow), cut into large pieces

1 red onion, cut into chunks

200g closed cup mushrooms

mint sauce

2 pitta breads

**Method**

Thread the pieces of lamb, pepper, onion and mushrooms onto soaked bamboo skewers. Brush with mint sauce and season with salt.

Cook on a ridged griddle pan over a medium heat, or under the grill, or on a barbecue preheated to medium-high heat. Cook, turning occasionally, for 12 to 15 minutes.

Heat the pitta breads briefly in the microwave. Once the kebabs are ready, place on the pitta and serve with extra mint sauce and a green salad.

**Recipe 13**

# Marinated Turkey Kebabs

Serves 4.    Prep 15 mins.
Cook 30 mins.

- **Ingredients**
- 1 (200g) tub 0% Greek yoghurt
- 100g feta cheese crumbled
- 2 tbsp fresh lemon juice
- 1/2 tsp lemon zest
- 2 tsp dried oregano
- ½ tsp salt
- ¼ tsp ground black pepper
- ¼ tsp crushed dried rosemary
- 500g skinless, boneless Turkey breast fillets - cut into 2.5cm pieces

- 1 large red onion, cut into wedges
- 1 large green pepper, cut into 3cm pieces
- 

**Method**

In a large shallow baking dish, mix the yoghurt, feta, lemon zest, lemon juice, oregano, salt, pepper and rosemary. Place the Turkey in the dish and turn to coat. Cover, and marinade for 3 hours in the fridge.

Preheat an outdoor barbecue to a high heat.

Thread the turkey, onion wedges and green pepper pieces alternately onto skewers. Discard the remaining yoghurt mixture.

BBQ the skewers until the turkey is no longer pink and the juices run clear.

**Recipe 14**

## Mini One Pot Dinners in Foil

### BBQ/oven

**Serves** 6. Prep 10 mins.

Cook 40 mins.

**Ingredients:**

6 large lamb chops

1 large onion, thinly sliced

3 carrots, thinly sliced

3 tomatoes, thinly sliced

6 medium potatoes, thinly sliced

**Method:**

(Set oven to 200C/Gas mark 6 if cooking on a stove)

Season the meat to individual tastes. Salt and pepper are fine if you don't have any other seasonings with you.

Place the meat in aluminium foil then layer with potatoes and veggies on top and wrap well.

Put the foil package in the oven or in coals and cook for 40 minutes.

**Suggestion**

Serve with a fresh salad in summer or steamed green vegetables in winter

**Recipe 15**

# Mr. Posh's BBQ Salmon

Serves 6.   Prep 15 mins.
Cook 30 mins.

- **Ingredients**
- 1 tbsp vegetable oil
- 1 tbsp soy sauce
- 1 tsp Worcestershire sauce
- Juice of 1 lemon
- 1/2 teaspoon grated fresh root ginger
- 2 tbsp honey
- 5 tbsp chopped fresh basil leaves
- 4 finely chopped shallots
- 6, 6 oz (175g) salmon fillet, with skin
- 
- 

**Method**

Make a pan out of aluminium foil by doubling up layers of foil large enough to hold your fillets. Place the foil onto a baking tray. Lay the fillets onto the foil with the skin side down. In a small bowl, stir together the oil, soy sauce, Worcestershire sauce, lemon juice, ginger, honey, basil and shallots. Pour over the salmon and let it marinate for about 20 minutes whilst you preheat the barbecue to a medium heat. Slide the foil with the salmon off the baking tray and onto the barbecue. Cover with the lid and barbecue the fillet for 10 minutes per 2.5cm (1 in) of thickness, about 20 minutes. The salmon should then be able to flake with a fork, but not be too dry. When you serve the salmon, the skin will stick to the foil and your barbecue will remain clean. Simply slice and use a spatula to scoop the fillet off the skin to serve

**Recipe 16**

## Pineapple Soy Chicken Skewers

Serves 10.   Prep 30 mins.

Cook 10 mins.

**Ingredients**

225ml pineapple juice

100g dark brown soft sugar

5 tbsp light soy sauce

1kg chicken breast mini fillets

Skewers (metal or bamboo)


**Method**

In a small saucepan over a medium heat, mix pineapple juice, sugar and soy

sauce. Remove from heat just before the mixture comes to the boil.

Place chicken in a medium bowl. Cover with the pineapple marinade and leave to cool for at least 30 minutes.

Preheat barbecue to medium heat.

Thread the chicken lengthwise onto the skewers and cook for 5 minutes each side or until the juices run clear.

They cook quickly, so watch them closely.

Serve with buttered crusty French rolls.

**Recipe 17**

## Porcini-Rubbed Steak

Serves 2.   Prep 15 mins.
Cook 5 mins.
Chill overnight.

### Ingredients

25g dried porcini mushrooms
1 sprig thyme, leaves only
2 thick sirloin steaks
1 tbsp olive oil
 baked potatoes and salad, to serve

### Method

Grind the mushrooms into a fine powder in a small food processor or coffee grinder or slice very thinly. Mix with a good pinch of salt, pepper and the thyme leaves. Rub the mixture all over the steaks. Then put onto a plate or into a sealable kitchen bag and chill overnight.

Brush away any excess mixture. Heat a griddle pan until smoking hot. Turn the heat to medium, then smear a little olive oil over one side of each steak. Griddle, oiled side down, for 3 mins. Turn over (there's no need to oil the other side), then cook for another 2 mins for medium-rare, or longer if you prefer medium or well done.

Serve with a baked potato and a salad.

**Recipe 18**

# Pork & Thyme Cheeseburgers

Prep 15 mins.    Cook 20 mins.
Makes 4 burgers.

- **Ingredients**
- 25g butter
- 1 onion, grated
- 500g pack lean pork mince
- 2 egg yolks
- 1 tbsp finely chopped thyme
- **To serve**
- 4 slices cheddar
- 4 tbsp chunky apple sauce
- 4 soft burger buns, split
- handful salad leaves and sliced tomatoes
- 

**Method**

Melt the butter in a small frying pan, add the onion and cook on a medium heat until soft and translucent, then cool. Put the pork into a large bowl and add the onion, egg yolks and thyme. Season well and mix together with your hands – don't overhandle or you will make the burgers tough. Divide the mixture into 4 and shape into burgers. Chill for 30 mins to firm up.

Heat the barbecue and cook the burgers for 10 mins each side. Top each burger with a slice of cheese, followed by 1 tbsp apple sauce, then return to the barbecue and close the lid, cooking for a further 5 mins to allow the cheese to melt. If your barbecue doesn't have a lid, loosely cover with foil, and toast the buns.

Serve the burgers in the buns with the salad leaves and sliced tomatoes.

**Recipe 19**

## Potato Salad with Broad Beans

Serves 4.   Prep 20 mins. Cook 30 mins.

- **Ingredients**
- 200g broad beans, fresh and podded, or frozen
- 750g salad potatoes
- 1 red onion, very thinly sliced
- 2 tbsp white wine vinegar
- ½ tsp sugar
- 150ml pot soured cream
- Bunch chives, snipped
- ½ tsp Dijon mustard
- 
- 

**Method**

Heat a pan of salted water and once boiling, add the broad beans. Bring the pan back to the boil for 2 mins, then lift the beans out with a slotted spoon into a bowl of cold water.

Put the potatoes into the pan, then boil for 15-20 mins or until tender. Drain and leave to cool.

While the potatoes are cooking, put the onion into a shallow bowl, splash with the vinegar and scatter over the sugar, then leave to soak. Pop the beans out of their jackets.

For the dressing, mix the soured cream, chives, mustard, 1 tbsp water and plenty of seasoning, measure 2 tsp of the vinegary juices from the onion, then stir to combine. Taste and add more of the vinegar if you like, then discard the rest. Cut the potatoes into halves or quarters and toss with the dressing and the onions.

Recipe 20

## Seared Steak with Chimichurri Dressing

Serves 2.   Prep 15 mins. Cook 8 mins, plus marinating.

- **Ingredients**
- 300g-400gpiece of lean rump or sirloin steak
- **For the dressing**
- 1 tsp cumin seeds
- ½ tsp fennel seeds
- small bunch flat-leaf parsley leaves, chopped
- 1 red chilli, deseeded and finely chopped
- 1 tsp thyme leaves
- 5 tbsp olive oil
- 2 tbsp red wine vinegar.

- **Method**
- To make the chimichurri dressing, toast the seeds in a small non-stick pan for 30 seconds or so, until they smell fragrant. Tip into a small bowl and stir in the chopped parsley, chilli, thyme, oil and vinegar. Season well with pepper – you can add salt just before serving.

- Put the steak onto a plate and rub over about a quarter of the dressing. Leave the steak marinating at room temperature for about 30 mins.
- If you're making ahead chill for up to 2 hrs, then bring out of the fridge about 15 mins before you want to cook it.
- Heat a barbecue, griddle or heavy based frying pan until very hot. Season the steak and dressing with salt, then cook the steak for 2-3 mins on each side depending on the thickness and how you like your meat cooked.
- Serve on a board, then slice into thin strips as you eat – spooning over the remaining dressing

Recipe 21

## Teriyaki BBQ Shrimp Skewers

Serves 4 to 6    Prep 15 mins. Cook 5-10 mins

- **Ingredients**
-
- 500g raw jumbo shrimps, peeled and deveined
- 1 fresh pineapple, peeled, cored, and cut into chunks
- 2 medium courgettes, cut into thick slices, then cut in half
- 3 red and orange peppers, cleaned and cut into small pieces
- Bamboo or metal skewers
- **For the Teriyaki BBQ Sauce:**
- 120g teriyaki sauce, store-bought or homemade
- 2 tbsp fish sauce
- 1-2 tbsp chili garlic sauce
-

**Method**

If using bamboo skewers, soak them in water while preparing the ingredients. Clean the shrimp.

Mix the Teriyaki BBQ Sauce ingredients in a bowl and add the shrimp to the marinade, while you chop the veggies and pineapple. Cut, slice, peel, and/or core vegetables and fruit as needed.

Heat the grill to 200C/Gas Mark 6. Slide pieces of the veggies, pineapple, and shrimp onto skewers in an alternating order as desired.

Brush the skewers with the Teriyaki BBQ Sauce you used to marinate the shrimp. Discard the remaining marinade. Grill 2-3 minutes each side, turning once. Serve warm.

## Snacks Index

1. Baked beans and Hash Brown Pasties

2. Corn Pancakes

3. Crab Sandwiches

4. Cucumber & Grape Side Salad

5. Date, Oat & Seed Treats

6. Egg Mayo & Watercress Rolls

7. Fishfinger Butty

8. Griddled Steak Sandwich

9. Homemade Fish Finger Sandwiches

10. Italian Style Soda Bread Rolls

11. Mr. Posh Salmon Egg Wraps

12. Mushroom & Cheese Burger

13. Ploughman's Roll

14. Prawn Cocktail Sandwich

15. Raspberry Brownies

16. Sandwich Filling

17.  Vegetable Club Sandwich

18.  Waffle with Avocado & Poached Eggs

**Recipe 1**

## Baked bean, sausage and hash brown pasties

Serves 4. Prep 15 mins.
Cook 40-45 mins.

**Ingredients**
Short crust pastry (shop bought)
Baked beans
4 rashers of bacon of your choice (Cut into 15mm squares)
4 Hash Browns
4 chipolata sausages sliced
1 egg
Olive oil.

- **Method**
- Heat oven 200c/180c fan/Gas Mark 6.
- Bake the hash browns on an oven tray for 20 minutes.
- Roll 500g short crust pastry into a large square.
- Cut four circles from the pastry using a side plate (about 20cm)
- Fry the bacon
- Slice 4 chipolata sausages and fry in 1 tsp oil until browned, then leave to cool.
- Divide the meat mixture and hash browns between the pastry circles.
- Spoon 3 tbsp baked beans into the center of each pastry circle
- Brush the pastry edges with beaten egg and fold over to cover the filling.

- Seal the edges with your thumb and fingers.
- Brush the top with more beaten egg.
- Bake for 20 to 25 mins or until golden.

**Recipe 2**

## Corn pancakes

Serves 4. Prep 10 mins.

Cook 5 mins.

**Ingredients:**

125g self-raising flour

4 eggs, beaten

15g chopped coriander

2 x 420g tins of sweet corn, drained

2 tbsp chopped chives

100g tasty cheese, grated

Butter, for frying

**Method:**

Place flour in a large mixing bowl and make a well in the centre.

Mix in the beaten eggs and milk. Fold in corn, chives and cheese.

Put ¼ cupful onto a medium heated and buttered frying pan.

Cook 2-3 minutes on each side until lightly browned. Keep warm.

Serve with a side salad and/or sweet chilli sauce

**Recipe 3**

## Crab Sandwiches

Makes 4 deep-filled sandwiches
Prep 20 mins.

### Ingredients

8 slices brown or granary bread, buttered
1 lemon, cut into 4 wedges, to serve

- **For the crab filling**

- brown crabmeat from 1 large brown crab, about 1½ kg in its shell (reserve the white meat, see below)
- 1 tbsp mayonnaise
- 1 tsp tomato ketchup
- juice of ½ lemon
- 1 tsp Dijon mustard
- big pinch cayenne pepper
  few drops brandy (if you have any)

- **For the white meat**
-
- white meat from the same crab
- small handful chopped mixed herbs such as parsley, dill, tarragon,
- chervil and chives
- juice ½ lemon
- 2 tbsp olive oil
-
- **Method**
-
- Make the crab filling: mix the ingredients together in a bowl and season, then set aside. In a separate bowl, mix the white meat with the herbs, lemon juice, oil and seasoning.
-
- Spread the bread lightly with butter, then spoon and spread the crab paste over 4 of the slices. Pile the white meat over, then top with the remaining bread. Cut the crusts off, if you like, and serve halved or in small triangles or squares with lemon wedges on the side.

**Recipe 4**

## Cucumber & grape side salad

Serves 6.  Prep 15-20 mins.

**Ingredients:**

2 cucumbers
1 large handful seedless grapes (green or red or both)
6-8 sprigs fresh mint leaves
2 tbsp balsamic vinegar
Juice of half a lemon
Half a chilli, sliced thinly

- **Method:**
-
- Slice cucumber into 1cm slices then into quarters.
- Slice grapes in half.
- Pick mint leaves and roughly bruise leaves or rip.
- Put all the above ingredients in a salad bowl.

- To make the salad dressing; mix lemon, balsamic vinegar and chilli together.
- Pour dressing on salad and toss.
- If required, using your hands, slightly squeeze the salad to let out some of the juices and then serve.
- (But do wash your hands after as the chilli makes your eyes smart if you rub your eyes after mixing)
- **Suggestion**
- If your children don't like chilli, you can strain the dressing to remove the chilli seeds or leave it out of the recipe altogether.

**Recipe 5**

## Date, oat & seed treats

Prep 10 mins.

Makes: 16

**Ingredients**

270g of dates roughly chopped

25g rolled oats

25g pistachios

25g mixed seeds

50g chopped almonds

**Method**

Place the dates, oats and pistachios in a food processor and blitz to give a paste. Add the seeds and pulse to mix.

Divide the paste into 16 and (with damp hands) form into balls. Roll in the chopped almonds, pressing the nuts into the date balls, and serve.

**Recipe 6**

## Egg Mayo & Watercress Rolls

Prep 10 mins.

Makes 10.

**Ingredients**

6 eggs

handful watercress, roughly chopped

8 tbsp good-quality mayonnaise

20 small assorted rolls

## Method

Hard-boil eggs for 10 mins, then drain and cool under cold water for 5 mins. Peel, roughly chop and put in a bowl.

Roughly chop the watercress and stir into the eggs with some salt, pepper and mayonnaise.

Divide the filling between the rolls.

Enjoy

Recipe 7

## Fishfinger Butty

**Northern style**

**Serves 1.   Prep 10 mins.**

**Cook 15-20 mins.**

## Ingredients

2 Slices of wholemeal seeded brown bread

4 Birdseye fishfingers

Butter

1 tsp of Tomato or Brown sauce

Salt & pepper if needed

**Method**

Grill the fishfingers until brown on both sides

Butter one side of the bread

Put sauce on the other slice

Put the cooked fishfingers on the buttered side, then the sauced slice on top, and press together.

**Recipe 8**

## Griddled steak sandwich

Serves 1.  Prop 10 mins. Cook 10 mins.

**Ingredients**
1 tbsp butter, soft
2 pitted olives, any colour
3 capers
pinch thyme leaves
175g rump steak, trimmed of any fat
2 tsp olive oil
olive oil
½ ciabatta loaf
2 little gem lettuces

**Method**
Put the butter in a small bowl and season with pepper. Finely chop the olives, capers and thyme leaves and stir into the butter. Chill until ready to use.

Heat a griddle pan or barbecue until smoking. Brush the steak with a little of the oil and cook for 3-4 mins each side, then transfer to a board and cover with foil to rest. Cut the ciabatta loaf in half, brush the cut side with remaining oil and place cut-side down on the griddle pan for 1-2 mins, until charred. Place the steak on the bottom half of the loaf and spoon the butter over it. Add the lettuce leaves and top with the other half of the ciabatta.

**Recipe 9**

## Homemade Fish Finger Sandwiches

Serves 4.  Prep 15 mins. Cook 35 mins.

- **Ingredients**
- 300g skinless white fish fillet
- 1 large egg, beaten
- 50g cornflakes, blitzed into crumbs
- 3 sweet potatoes, cut into chunky chips
- 1 tbsp olive oil
- 4 small wholemeal buns
- small handful mixed salad leaves
- 1 lemon, cut into wedges
- **For the tartare sauce**
- 2 tbsp light mayonnaise
- 1 tbsp gherkins
- 1 tsp capers
- Capers, rinsed and chopped
-

**Method**

Heat oven to 200C/180C fan/Gas Mark 6. Cut the fish into 4 equal-sized portions, dip in the beaten egg and coat in cornflakes, then chill for 10 mins. Put the sweet potatoes on an oiled baking tray and season, then cook for 20 mins on a baking tray.

Meanwhile, make the tartare sauce. Mix all the ingredients with some seasoning, then set aside.

Remove the sweet potato chips, turn them over, add the fish to the tray and cook everything for 15 mins more, turning the fish halfway through. When cooked, add a few salad leaves to each bun, top with the fish and a splash of tartare sauce, and serve with the chips and lemon wedges.

Recipe 10

## Italian style soda bread rolls

Serves 4.   Prep 10 mins.

Cook 35 mins.

**Ingredients:**

250g self-raising flour

2 tsp baking powder

Pinch salt

60g cheddar cheese, grated

75g sun-dried tomatoes, chopped

Good sprinkling Italian herbs

8 Sliced & pitted black olives

125g Milk

**Method:**

In a large bowl, mix together flour, baking powder, salt, tomatoes, olives, cheese and herbs.

Add in enough milk to make soft wet dough.

Divide into four portions and place on a well-greased floured tray.

Cook in a preheated oven at 200C/Gas Mark 6 for about 35 mins.

**Suggestion.**   Cut open and spread garlic cream cheese thickly.

**Recipe 11**

# Mr. Posh's Salmon & egg wraps

Prep 20 mins.
Makes 12

**Ingredients**
24 slices smoked salmon room temperature
6 hard-boiled eggs, cooled, shelled and sliced
2 x 100g bags baby spinach
12 large wraps, I used multigrain

**For the mustard mayo**
200g light mayonnaise
tbsp Dijon mustard
1 small red onion, very finely sliced
Mix the mayonnaise and mustard, divide into 2 small bowls, then stir the onion into one bowl.

**Method**

To assemble, spread a layer of the onion mayonnaise over each wrap and add 2 slices of salmon, some sliced hard-boiled egg and a generous helping of spinach to each. Roll up tightly.

The wraps can be made several hours ahead and kept covered in the fridge. To serve, cut each wrap on the diagonal into 2 pieces. Serve with the extra mustard mayo for drizzling.

Enjoy

**Recipe 12**

## Mushroom & Cheese Burger

Serves  4     Prep 10 mins. Cook 20-25 mins.

- **Ingredients:**
- 
- 50g cheddar cheese, grated
- 1 tin sliced mushrooms, drained
- 76g mayonnaise
- 6 slices bacon, cooked and crumbled or chopped
- 1 onion, finely chopped
- ½ tsp salt
- ½ tsp pepper
- ¼ tsp garlic powder
- ⅛ tsp chilli sauce
- 500 g lean mince
- 4 Burger buns
-

**Method:**

In a bowl, combine the cheese, mushrooms, mayo, and bacon.
Cover and refrigerate.
In another bowl, combine onion, salt, garlic powder and pepper.
Add mince and mix well. Shape into patties.
Grill covered over medium-hot heat for 4-5 minutes on each side.
Spoon the cheese mixture on top of each burger.
Grill until cheese begins to melt.
Lettuce and tomato if desired
TIP: You can prepare these in advance and freeze until required.

**Recipe 13**

# Ploughman's Rolls

Prep 40 mins.   Cook 20-25 mins. Makes 8

**Ingredients**
1 tbsp celery
Celery seeds, plus a few extra
500g pack bread dough
200ml milk, plus a splash to glaze
100g extra-mature cheddar, grated
85g English Brie or camembert, diced
1 small apple, cored and diced into small chunks
2 spring onions, finely chopped
1 tbsp poppy seeds
plain flour, for dusting
pickle, to serve

**Method**
Stir the celery seeds into the bread dough mix. Pour the milk into a jug, make up to 325ml with water, then warm to hand temperature (this is easy to do in the microwave). Add to the bread mix and bring together following the pack instructions. Leave to rise in a warm place until about doubled in size.
Meanwhile, mix together 85g of the cheddar, the Brie, apple and spring onions, and season a little.

Divide the dough into 8 even pieces. Roll a piece into a roughly 10cm-wide circle (about the thickness of a naan), then spoon an eighth of the cheesy mixture into the middle. Gather up the edges of the dough around the filling and pinch together to seal firmly (you don't want it to burst while baking.) Turn the roll over so the pinched bit seals and squashes together underneath. Re-shape a little if necessary. Repeat with the remaining dough and filling, then put onto floured baking sheets, spaced a little apart. Cover with oiled cling film and set aside in a warm place for 30 mins more.

Heat the oven to 200C/180C fan/Gas Mark 6. Brush the rolls with a splash of milk, scatter with the poppy seeds plus a pinch more celery seeds and the remaining cheddar, then bake for 20-25 mins. Eat warm or cold, with pickle.

**Recipe 14**

## Prawn Cocktail Sandwich

Serves 2. Prep 15 mins.

**Ingredients**

2 tbsp extra-light mayonnaise

1 tbsp reduced-sugar ketchup

2 tbsp chopped dill

1 lemon, cut into 8 wedges

100g pack cooked and peeled North Atlantic prawns

½ cucumber, deseeded and diced

2 handfuls cherry tomatoes, halved

20g bag rocket

4 slices wholemeal bread

## Method

Make the dressing in a medium bowl. Mix the mayonnaise, ketchup, half the dill, the juice from 4 of the lemon wedges and some seasoning. Put in the prawns, cucumber and tomatoes.

Arrange the bread on 2 plates, top each with rocket and pile on the prawn filling. Scatter with remaining dill and serve with the remaining lemon wedges.

Place unbuttered/ unsauced slice on top and press.

Recipe 15

# Raspberry brownies.

Prep 10 mins.   Cook 30-35 mins. Makes: 20 squares.
•Ingredients
•200g Continental Plain Chocolate, broken into pieces
100g Belgian Milk Chocolate, broken into pieces
250g unsalted butter, diced
400g light brown sugar
4 medium British Free-Range Eggs, beaten
175g plain flour
25g cocoa powder
150g pack Raspberries
2 tbsp flaked almonds

•Method

- Preheat the oven to 180°C/Gas mark 4. Line a 20 x 30cm baking tin with baking parchment.

- Put the chocolate, butter and sugar in a saucepan and heat gently, stirring, until melted and smooth. Remove from the heat then gradually beat in the eggs until well mixed.
- Sieve the flour and cocoa then gently stir in. Add half the raspberries and almonds, then spoon into the prepared tin. Scatter over the remaining raspberries and almonds and bake for 30–35 minutes until just set.
- Leave to cool in the tin for 5 minutes then turn out onto a wire rack and leave to cool completely. Cut into 20 squares and store in the fridge if not eating the same day.
- **Tip**
- Serve the brownies warm with a scoop of vanilla ice cream for a delicious dessert

Recipe 16

## Sandwich Filling

Serves 2.   Prep 10 mins. Cook 20 mins.

**Ingredients:**

1 onion

1 tomato

1 tbsp butter

2 tbsp grated cheese

1 egg, beaten

½ tsp mixed herbs

Salt and pepper

**Method:**

Peel the onion and tomato and cut into small pieces, then cook in a saucepan with the butter.

Add salt and pepper to taste.

When tender, add the grated cheese, beaten egg and a good pinch of mixed herbs.

Cook until the mixture thickens

Suggestion:

This mixture can be used as a delicious filling for sandwiches or served on a cheese and cracker platter, or add cooked meat, ham, corned beef.

Leftovers can be kept in the fridge for up to three days.

**Recipe 17**

# Vegetarian club sandwich

Serves 1.    Total time: 10 minutes

Ingredients

75g kale

2 tsp French dressing

3 slices Farmhouse Batch Multi Seeded Bread, toasted

50g coleslaw

50g houmous

25g vegetarian Cheddar cheese, grated

Method

Cook the kale in boiling water for 4 minutes, drain and run under cold water. Remove any thick stalks and squeeze out excess liquid. Mix with the dressing and place on top of 1 slice of toast. Top this with coleslaw.

Spread another slice of toast with houmous and sprinkle over the cheese, place on top of the coleslaw. Top with the remaining slice of toast and cut in half. Serve with a few crisps and a handful of salad.

**Recipe 18**

## Waffle with avocado and poached eggs

Serves          Prep 15 mins.   Cook 30 mins.

**Ingredients**
1 red onion, cut into thin rings
1 tsp plain flour
olive oil cooking spray
splash malt vinegar
4 eggs
1 large ripe avocado
½ lime, juiced
**For the waffle**
1 egg
150g self-raising flour
250ml milk
1 tsp baking powder
½ tsp smoked paprika
75g butter, melted

**Method**

Preheat the oven to 200°C/ 180°Cfan/Gas Mark 6. Put the onion with the flour in a bowl and season, then put on a non-stick baking tray and spray with the oil. Bake for 10-12 mins until crisp.

To make the waffle, whisk together the egg, flour, milk, baking powder, paprika and a pinch of salt. Heat a griddle pan and brush with butter. Stir the remaining butter into the waffle mixture until combined. Pour into the pan, then cook for 5 mins until golden brown. Turn and cook for a further 3-4 mins, until cooked through.

Meanwhile, heat a pan of water to a simmer. Add the vinegar and swirl. Add 2 eggs and poach for 3 mins. Drain on kitchen paper and keep warm. Repeat with the other 2 eggs.

In a bowl, mash the avocado flesh with the lime juice, then season.

Divide the waffle into 4 and spread each quarter with avocado. Top with an egg and some crispy onions.

# How to Basic Cook

1. Mashed Potato

2. Courgette & Tomato Chutney

3. Dice an Onion

4. Double Pod Broad Beans

5. Fillet a Fish

6. Joint a Whole Chicken into Eight Pieces

7. Kernel Sweetcorn

8. Buttered Cabbage

9. Basic Pastry

10. Basic Sweet Pastry

11. Pastry for Savoury Pies

12.   Roost Potatoes

13.   How to make Salsa

14.   Buttered Garlic Cabbage

15.   Cheese Base Pizza Pastry

16.   Cheesy Garlic Mashed Potatoes

17.   How to Make Eggnog

18.   Garlic Potatoes

19.   How to make Harissa Paste

20.   How to make Hidden Vegetable Sauce

21.   How to make Perfect Rice

22.   Shortcrust Pastry

23.   Peel a Tomato

24.   Peel Peppers

25.   Poach an Egg

26.   Prepare a Mango

27.   Prepare a Pineapple

28.   Prepare a Pomegranate

29.   Prepare a Whole Salmon

30.   Prepare an Avocado

31.   Prepare Leeks

32.   Prepare Papaya

33.   To Shuck or Open Oysters

34.   How to Wilt Spinach

35.   No-Lump White Sauce

36.   Cheesy White Sauce

37.   Four Cheese Sauce

38.   Onion Bechamel Sauce

39.   Spicy Tomato Sauce

**Recipe 1**

## How to make.  Basic Mashed Potatoes

Potatoes are blended with melted butter and milk to create perfectly smooth mashed potatoes.
Serves 4.   Prep 15 mins.
Cook 20 mins.
**Ingredients**
900g baking potatoes, peeled and quartered
2 tablespoons butter
40ml milk, or as needed
salt and pepper to taste

**Method**

Bring a pot of salted water to the boil. Add the potatoes and cook for about 15 minutes until tender but still firm, then drain.

In a small saucepan heat the butter and milk over a low heat until the butter has melted. Using a potato masher or electric beaters, slowly blend milk mixture into potatoes until smooth and creamy. Season with salt and pepper to taste .

**Cheat tip,**

use only the saucepan that the potatoes are in, once you have drained the potatoes return the pan to the heat and add the butter and milk, remove from the heat once the butter has melted and mash or blend.

**Recipe 2**

## How to make. Courgette & Tomato Chutney

Prep 20 mins.    Cook 2 hrs 45 mins.
Makes approx. 2.5kg.

**Ingredients**
500ml cider vinegar or white wine vinegar
400g brown sugar (any brown sugar will work)
1 tbsp mixed spice
2 tbsp yellow mustard seeds
1 cinnamon stick
4 onions chopped
1kg courgettes, diced
1kg tomatoes, chopped
4 eating apples, peeled and diced

300g sultanas

**Method**
Put the vinegar, 300ml water, sugar and spices in a very large pan. Heat, stirring until the sugar dissolves then add the rest of the ingredients with a tsp of salt.
Bring back to a simmer, then simmer uncovered for 2 ½hours until darkened, thick and chutney-like.
To sterilise the jars, wash thoroughly in very hot soapy water. Rinse in very hot water then put on a baking sheet in a 140C/fan 120C/gas 1 oven until completely dry.
Pour the chutney into the sterilised jars while still hot, seal and leave in a cool dark place for at least 3 weeks before opening.

Recipe 3

# How to Dice an Onion

Try freezing onions for 20 minutes before chopping them, to stop your eyes from watering. Once cut, an onion should be wrapped, refrigerated and used within 4 days.

**Step 1**
Cut the onion in half, slicing downwards through the root, then peel.

**Step 2**
Cut 5-6 vertical slices into each half, leaving the root intact.

**Step 3**
Lay the onion half flat, slicing horizontally and keeping the root intact.

**Step 4**
Slice downwards across these cuts to dice.

Recipe 4

# How to Double-Pod Broad Beans

Broad beans can be eaten complete with their greeny-grey skins, but they're much nicer and prettier double podded to reveal the bright green jewels inside.

**Step 1**
First remove the beans from their pods.

**Step 2**
Bring a small saucepan of water to the boil and add the beans. Cook for approximately 2 minutes and then drain.

**Step 3**

Place the beans into a bowl of cold water.

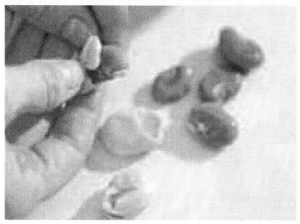

**Step 4**

Pop the tender, bright green beans out of their thick, leathery skins by squeezing gently.

Recipe 5

## How to Fillet a Fish

Follow this step-by-step guide on the simplest way to fillet a fish, and learn what the best tools for the job are.

Essential kitchen kit

Filleting knife - A knife with a flexible blade allows you to move easily between the flesh and bones of the fish - and the sharper the knife the easier the job.

Scissors - You'll need sharp scissors to snip off the fins.

### Need to know

This is the most effective way to fillet round fish such as sea bass, mackerel, trout, sea bream, john dory, cod, pollock, mullet, salmon and sardines. Ask your fishmonger to scale the fish for you.

**Step 1** - Put the scaled fish on a chopping board and, using scissors, trim off the fins by the head on each side, and any fins that run along the top and on the underside of the fish.

**Step 2** - With the tip of the knife, pierce the stomach of the fish using the small hole by the tail as a guide. Run the knife from the tail to the head, cutting open the stomach. Clean out the contents of the stomach and rinse the fish in cold running water.

**Step 3** - Return the fish to the chopping board and make a long cut around the head and just below the gills on both sides: remove the head.

**Step 4** - Tail towards you, run the knife down the spine to the tail in a gentle slicing - not sawing - action, working the blade between the spine and the flesh. Repeat until the fillet begins to come away - lift the fillet to see where you're working.

**Step 5** - When you get to the rib bones, let the knife follow the shape of the fish and slice over the bones. Once you've removed the fillet, set it aside.

**Step 6** - Turn over the fish and repeat with the second fillet, this time starting at the tail and working towards the head. Be careful - the second fillet may be a little trickier to remove.

**Recipe 6**

## How to Joint a Chicken into Eight Pieces

As whole chickens are often the same price as a couple of breast pieces, it makes sense to know how to joint a chicken yourself and use the portions you don't need in other dishes. Cooking with joints that include bones rather than boneless portions will also result in a much more delicious sauce.

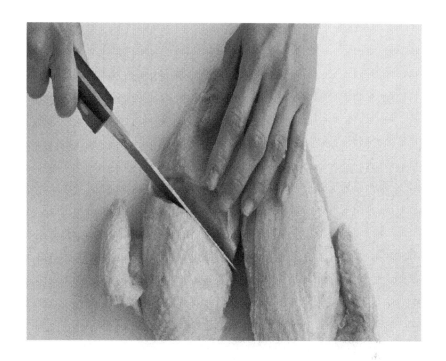

...Joint a chicken into eight pieces
Step by step

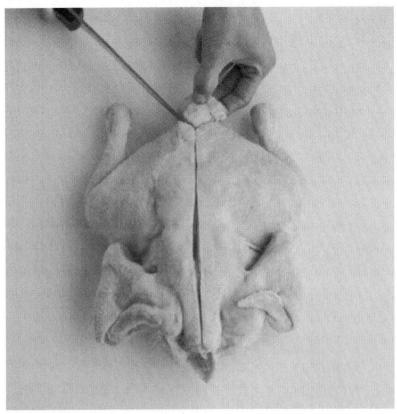

**1** Cutting either side of the parson's nose.

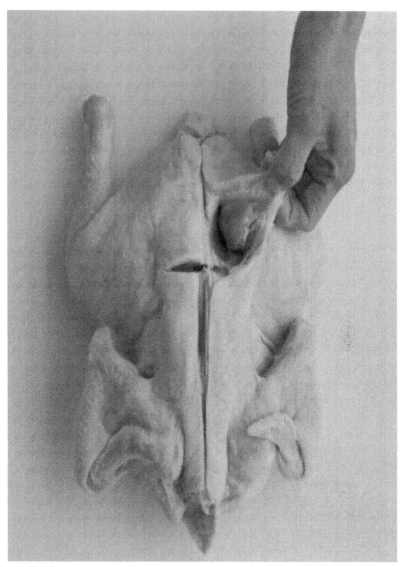

2 Releasing the oysters.

**3** Cutting between the drumstick and breast to the joint holding the thigh to the carcass.

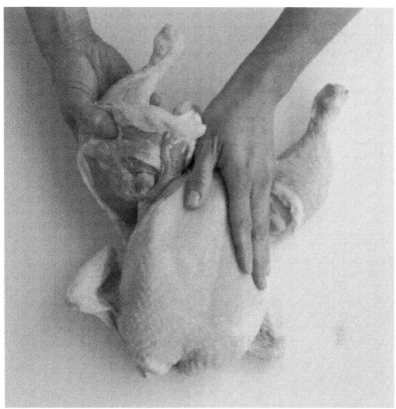

4 Pulling the thigh/leg back to release it from the carcass.

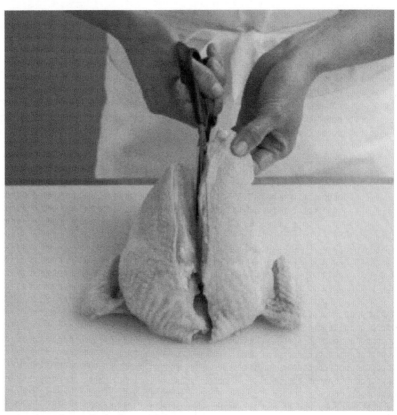

**5** Cutting through the breast bone.

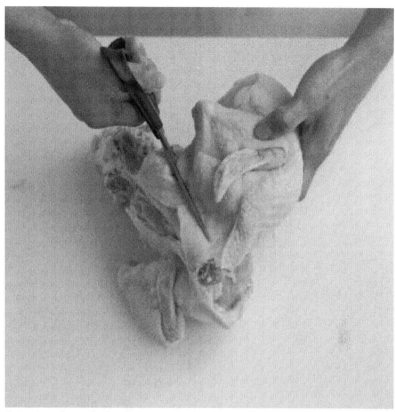

**6** Cutting through the ribs.

7 Cutting through the thigh/leg to divide in two.

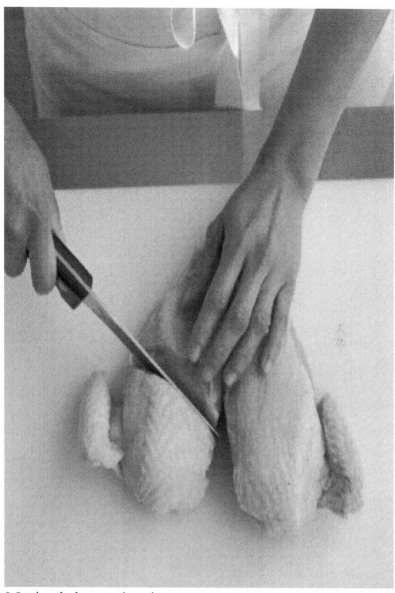

8 Cutting the breasts pieces in two.

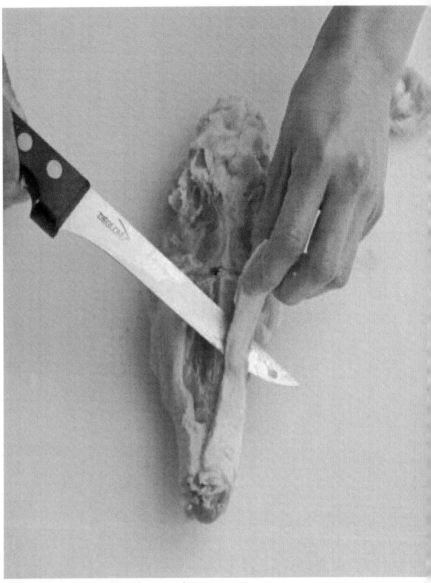

**9** Trimming the carcass of excess fat.

**Instructions**

1.  Place the chicken breast side down on a board with the neck end away from you. Make a cut through the skin, down the middle of the carcass, from the neck end to just above the parson's nose. Make a cut on either side of the parson's nose.

2.  Identify the oysters, which lie on the carcass at the top of the thigh. Make a cut across the top of the oysters, then release the sinew holding the oysters in place with your knife and release the oysters with your thumb.

3. Now turn the chicken so it is breast side uppermost, still with the neck end away from you. Pull the skin over the breast to ensure it is fully covered. Cut between the drumstick and breast, keeping the knife close to the breast, but on the outside of the carcass bone at the entrance to the cavity, until the joint holding the thigh to the carcass is exposed. Do the same on the other side. Place your fingers under the thigh and your thumb on top of it and push up with your fingers to 'pop' the thigh joint. Repeat on the other side.

4. Tilt the chicken to one side, pulling the thigh/leg backwards towards the carcass, helping to expose the oyster. Release the oyster using a knife and continue to pull back the thigh/leg. You will need to release the tendons holding the thigh bone to the carcass. Once this is done, pull the thigh/leg back towards you to release the joint from the carcass. Repeat on the other side and put the thigh/leg pieces on one side.

5. Now turn the chicken breast side uppermost and stretch the skin over the breast. Cut down one side of the breast bone – either side will do, but not both – until the knife blade encounters the bone. Use a pair of kitchen or poultry scissors to cut through the breast bone completely.

6. Put the chicken on its side and from the point of the breast, using the scissors, cut through the ribs following the fat line around the wing and through the wing joint. Repeat on the other side; it might be easier to start at the wing end.

7. Now the 4 pieces need to be divided again. Place the leg/thigh pieces skin side down on the board and, using your knife, cut through the joint, using the fat line covering the joint as a guide. If the knife meets the bone, move the knife a little to the left or right and try again. It should cut cleanly through the joint. Repeat with the second leg/thigh piece.

8. To divide the breast pieces, tuck the attached wing tips behind them, then take an imaginary line from the bottom of the wing to the 'cleavage'. Cut through the meat with your knife, then through the bone with a pair of scissors to leave a diamond shaped tapering piece of breast and a smaller, but thicker, piece with the wing attached. Trim off the end wing pinion. The chicken should now have been jointed into 8 pieces.

9. The carcass can be trimmed of excess fat and used for making stock.

### Recipe 7
## How to Kernel Sweetcorn

Fresh sweetcorn is a delicious way to perk up summer salads. Barbecuing or grilling the cobs, with their tightly-packed kernels, brings out their naturally sweet flavour.

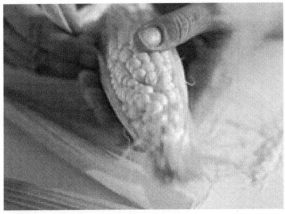

**Step 1**
Remove the husk and 'silk' from the corn.

**Step 2**

Brush with vegetable oil and barbecue or grill for 10-15 minutes, turning regularly.

**Step 3**

Trim one end of the cob to create a flat surface, then stand on its end. Using a sharp knife, carefully cut off the corn kernels from top to bottom.

**Step 4**

Add to a salad.

**Recipe 8**

## How to make "Buttered Cabbage"

Serve 6- 8 servings.    Prep 10 mins.


Cook 25 mins.


**Ingredients**


1 lb fresh Savoy cabbage

2-4 tbsp butter

salt and freshly ground pepper

an extra knob of butter

**Method**


Remove all the tough outer leaves from the cabbage. Cut the cabbage into four, remove the stalk and then cut each quarter into fine shreds, working across the grain. Put 2 or 3 tablespoons of water into a wide saucepan, together with the butter and a pinch of salt. Bring to a boil, add the cabbage and stir in over a high heat, then cover the saucepan and cook for a few minutes. Stir again and add some salt, freshly ground pepper and the knob of butter. Drain and serve immediately.

Recipe 9

## How to make Basic Pastry

Prep 10 mins.

**Ingredients**

1 egg

120ml milk

225 g butter/margarine

I pinch of salt

200/250 g plain flour (if you require the pastry to rise use self-rising flour)

**Method**

Put the flour and butter/margarine in a large bowl and by hand rub the mix together until your mix resembles breadcrumbs.

Whisk the egg and add the milk together with a pinch of salt and pour into the flour mix stirring with a wooden spoon until the mix becomes dough.

Use your hands to knead the dough, adding flour as needed to make a pliable non-sticky dough (if sticky add more flour slowly)

Place on a floured board and roll out to the dimension you require, and if the rolling pin sticks rub a little more flour on.

**Tip**

I use stork margarine

**Recipe 10**

## How to make Basic Sweet Pastry

This sweet shortcrust pastry freezes beautifully so you can prepare it in advance if you wish to make a few pies or tarts while you are away in the caravan /motorhome.

Serves 16

Prep 10 mins.

- **Ingredients**
    - 225g unsalted butter, chilled
    - 375g plain flour
    - 3 tablespoons caster sugar
    - 80ml iced water (if not iced cold water will suffice, or cold Milk)
    - 

**Method**

Prep: 15min, Extra time: 30min chilling, Ready in: 45min

Combine flour and sugar in the bowl of an electric stand mixer. Cut butter into tablespoon-sized pieces; add it to the flour and butter. Use the paddle beater to mix the butter and flour together. you are trying to achieve a bread crumb mix. Alternatively, if you decide to try this in the van you can do it by hand with a fork. Or mixed by hand you are trying to achieve a bread crumb mix.

With the mixer on low speed or while stirring the mixture with a fork, pour in the cold water. When the dough starts to clump, and before it turns into a ball, stop stirring.

Lightly knead dough in the bowl until it forms a ball. Divide dough into two parts. Flatten each part into a disc and chill for about 30 minutes before rolling.

**Recipe 11**

# How to make Pastry for Savoury Pies

Prep time 25 min
This is my basic shortcrust pastry recipe that I use for savoury pies, tarts and quiches. Compared to traditional shortcrust pastry, this is much simpler to make as it calls for olive oil instead of butter.

**Ingredients**
Makes: 2 tart cases (a 20cm casing will generously feed four)
1 egg
120ml warm milk
60ml extra virgin olive oil = 4 table spoons
1 pinch salt
200 to 250g plain flour = 13 to 16 tablespoons
Prep:10min > Extra time:15min chilling > Ready in:25min

Method

Whisk egg, warm milk and olive oil together in a large bowl; season with salt. Add 200g flour, in batches, mixing well until the dough is formed and adding additional flour if needed.

Remove pastry dough from bowl and place on lightly floured surface; knead lightly until smooth. Wrap in cling film and chill in the fridge for 15 minutes. After chilling, dough is ready to be used.

No need to over knead

Don't knead too much, otherwise the gluten will react and you won't get the flaky texture you are looking for.

**Recipe 12**

## How to make Roast Potatoes

For gloriously crisp edges, the key is to give your pan a good shake after par-boiling to rough up the edges of the roast potatoes
Prep 10 mins
Cook time 30/35 minutes

### What you'll need:
120g duck fat
1.5kg floury potatoes (such as maris piper), peeled and cut into chunks

### How to cook

Preheat the oven to 180°C, gas mark 4; put the fat in a roasting tin and heat in the oven. Place the peeled potatoes in a pan and just cover with salted cold water. Bring to the boil, then reduce the heat and simmer for 5 minutes. Drain and leave in the pan for 2-3 minutes to steam-dry, then shake the pan to roughen them up.

Carefully transfer the potatoes to the roasting tin, turning in the hot fat and leaving plenty of space between each one. Sprinkle with sea salt and roast for 30 minutes, turning halfway through.

Turn up the oven to 220°C/Gas Mark 7, and roast for 30 minutes more, again turning halfway, until crisp and golden, and ready to serve.

**Recipe 13**

## How to make Salsa

Serves 4.    Prep less than 30 mins.

No cooking.

**Ingredients**

250g fresh tomatoes, finely chopped

1 small onion, finely chopped

3 mild chillies, finely chopped

bunch coriander, finely chopped

salt, to taste

lime juice, to taste

1 tbsp water

**Method**

To make the salsa, combine all the ingredients together in a bowl and serve immediately.

**Recipe 14**

## How to make Buttered Garlic Cabbage

Serves 6     Prep 5 mins.

Cook 10 mins.

**INGREDIENTS**

2 tbsp sunflower oil

25g butter

2 garlic cloves, finely chopped

1 large savoy cabbage, outer leaves discarded, cored and shredded

**METHOD**

Heat the oil and butter in a large saucepan. Add the garlic and heat for 20 seconds. Stir in the cabbage and 2 tablespoons water. Season, cover and cook over a medium heat for 10 minutes, stirring now and then, until wilted and very tender.

Serve as a side dish

**Recipe 15**

## How to make Cheese Based Pizza

Prep 15 mins.

Cook 5 mins.

**For the base**

250g self-raising flour

2 oz Cheese grated

150ml milk

35g butter (Use Garlic butter if you prefer)

**Method**

Mix the flour, milk cheese and butter in a bowl – rub in by hand to create a breadcrumb type mix, it should come together as a dough, but if it is too wet add a little flour.

Flour your work surface and put the dough on it, knead it lightly to bring all the bits together then lay it out on a floured work top - roll the dough out to a 10-inch pizza size and place on a floured baking tray.

Cook on 190C/Gas Mark 5 for about 5 minutes just to help it take the topping without going soggy

When browned add the toppings of your choice.

**Recipe 16**

## How to make Cheesy Garlic Mashed Potatoes

Serves 4.   Prep 10 mins.

Cook 15-20 mins.

### Ingredients

5 medium potatoes, peeled and diced

2 cloves of garlic, minced (use a garlic press)

200g grated Cheddar cheese

50g butter or margarine or garlic butter

### Method

Bring a saucepan of salted water to the boil. Add the potatoes and garlic and cook for about 15 minutes then drain.

In a small saucepan heat the butter and milk over low heat until butter is melted.

Add the cheese scattering it into the mash then add the milk mix

Using a potato masher or electric beaters, slowly blend milk mixture into potatoes until smooth and creamy. Season with salt and pepper to taste.

Recipe 17

## How to make, Eggnog

Prep 10 mins.

Cook 10 mins.

Even though eggnog is associated with North America as a quirky Christmas tradition, it is rumoured to have come from Europe, and possibly even England.

The sheer mention is often enough to cause people to wince, presumably because alcohol and milk sounds like a recipe for disaster, but it's a tradition for a reason, and done right, can make a delicious and fun twist to your Christmas party.

**Here's a step by step guide on how to make a classic eggnog that even the Grinch will enjoy!**

**Steps:**

1. Put 25ml brandy, 20ml dark rum, a dash of sugar syrup and 1 medium egg into a shaker and fill with ice.

2. Shake and strain into a saucepan.

3. Add 75ml of milk and simmer on a low heat. Don't allow it to boil. Wait a few minutes and you are ready to serve.

4. Sprinkle with nutmeg just before serving.

**Recipe 18**

## How to make Garlic Potatoes.

Serves       Prep 10 mins

Cook 60 mins.

Sit 750g new potatoes in the middle of a large sheet of foil on a baking tray.

Dot with 50g garlic butter and season well. Seal the sides of the foil to make a parcel.

Roast at 200C/180C fan/Gas Mark6 for 1 hr.

Open the foil with care as it will very hot and toss the potatoes in their butter.

Recipe 19

# How to make Harissa Paste

Making your own Harissa paste is incredibly easy and once you taste it, you won't be able to stop using it. Perfect as a marinade for meat or a fiery dressing for roasted vegetables.
Prep Time 10 mins, Cook Time 5 mins, Total Time 15 minutes

### Ingredients
2 x red peppers/sweet pimento peppers charred, and skins removed
5 peeled garlic cloves
1 x 400g can chopped tomatoes (include the juice for a saucier consistency)
1 tablespoon smoked paprika
2 x fresh red chillies
1 x fresh red bird's eye chilli
5-6 tablespoons olive oil
salt & black pepper to taste
### for the spice mix
1 teaspoon cumin seeds
1 teaspoon fennel seeds
2 teaspoons coriander seeds
2 teaspoons dried chilli flakes

### Method
Toast all the spices (in the spice mix) over medium heat in a pan until fragrant. Grind in a pestle & mortar until fine and set aside.

In a blender/food processor, combine all the remaining ingredients along with the spices then blend well until you have a brick-red, vibrant paste. Season to taste then transfer to jars.

Recipe 20

## How to make, Hidden Vegetable Sauce

Prep 20 mins.    Cook 55 mins.

- **Ingredients**
- 1 leek (chopped roughly)
- 2 courgettes (chopped into chunks)
- 1 red pepper (or yellow pepper, coarsely chopped)
- 8 mushrooms, chopped
- 1 small aubergine (chopped into chunks)
- 1 garlic clove crushed
- 2 x 400g tins chopped tomatoes
- Pinch dried oregano
- pepper (to taste)
- sugar (optional)
- 1 tbsp olive oil (or butter)
- 
- **Method**
- In a little olive oil or butter, add all the vegetables and garlic and soften gently for about 10 minutes
- Add the tins of tomatoes and sprinkle on the herbs, pepper and sugar
- Stir to combine, then cover and simmer for about 30-45 minutes
- Once all the vegetables are completely soft, transfer the mixture to a blender – or use a handheld blender – and blitz it until moderately smooth
- Spoon into ice cube trays or small pots and freeze
- The recipe makes a large volume of sauce – but you'll get through it as it's very versatile
- Note
- Can be used as a compliment to an all English breakfast and BBQ meats

**Recipe 21**

# How to Cook Perfectly Fluffy Rice Every Time

Prep time 10 mins, Cook time 20 minutes

## Ingredients

- 200g long grain or basmati rice
- ½ tsp salt
- 600ml cold water

## Method

Weigh the rice and tip into a sieve. Wash the rice under running cold water until it runs clear. This will rinse off excess starch to ensure that the cooked rice is not sticky.

Shake off the water and tip the rice into a medium-sized saucepan. Add half a teaspoon of salt and 600ml cold water. Bring to the boil, then give the rice a stir and reduce the heat. Cover with the lid and cook for 10 minutes.

Take a look at the rice. The water should have been absorbed. If it is not, cover again and cook for a further 2-3 minutes. Turn off the heat and leave the rice, covered, for 5 minutes. This will drive off any excess moisture to ensure the grains are fluffy and separate.

Fluff up the rice with a fork before serving.

Recipe 22

## How to make, Shortcrust Pastry

**Ready in:40min**
This recipe provides the wrapping or covering for many pies and tarts, both sweet and savoury. Follow individual recipe instructions for methods of use and baking. See notes at the bottom of recipe for more ideas. This recipe makes enough to line a deep 20-23cm (8-9 inch) flan tin or to cover a large pie dish for serving 4-6.

- **Ingredients**
  **Serves: 6**
- 170 g plain flour
- pinch of salt
- 85 g cool butter, diced
- Cool or iced water

**Method**

Sift the flour and salt into a large mixing bowl. Add the butter and rub into the flour until the mixture resembles breadcrumbs.
Sprinkle with 3 tbsp of cold water and mix in using a round-bladed knife. Add a drop more water only if the dough will not clump together. With your hands, gather together into a firm but pliable dough, handling as little as possible, wrap the ball of dough in greaseproof paper or cling film and chill for at least 30 minutes before rolling out.

**Some more ideas.** For spiced shortcrust, add 1 tsp ground spice to the flour (such as cumin, curry powder, cinnamon or ginger). * For herbed shortcrust, add 1 tbsp finely chopped fresh herbs or 1 tsp dried herbs to the flour.

Recipe 23

## How to Peel a Tomato

Skinless tomatoes are easy to prepare and perfect for making tomato sauce.

**Method**

Using a sharp knife, lightly score the base of the tomatoes with a cross.

Place the tomatoes in a pan or bowl and cover with freshly boiled water. Leave for 3-4 minutes, or until the skins begin to wrinkle and split.

Plunge the tomatoes into a bowl of iced water to reduce their temperature.

Carefully peel away the skins with your fingers.

Juicy English tomatoes are versatile and can be enjoyed in many ways.

**Recipe 24**

## How to Peel Peppers

Peeling peppers this way gives them a smooth texture and concentrated flavour. They're great added to salads or pasta sauces or serve them as an antipasto.

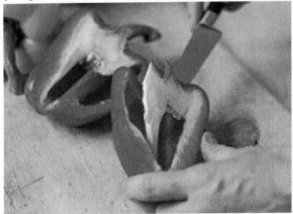

**Step 1**
Cut the peppers in half and remove the stalk, seeds and white membrane.

**Step 2**

Place the peppers under a hot grill, skin side up, turning as the skin blackens.

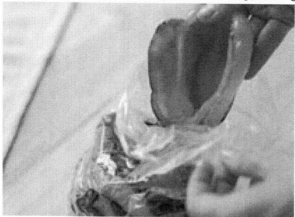

**Step 3**

Seal in a plastic bag and leave to cool

**Step 4**

Remove the peppers from the bag. The skin should now peel away

**Recipe 25**

## How to Poach an Egg

A perfectly poached egg is delicious served with fishcakes or smoked haddock, or simply on buttered toast. For best results, use fresh eggs.

### Step 1

Pour boiling water into a shallow pan or frying pan, to a depth of about 3cm Bring back to the boil then reduce to a simmer.

## Step 2

Crack each egg into a cup, then gently tip into the water. Cook no more than 2 or 3 eggs at a time.

## Step 3

Keep the water simmering for about a minute, until each egg white is opaque.

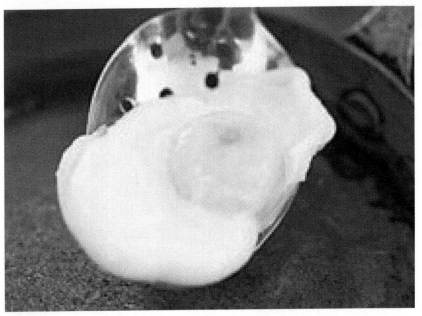

## Step 4

Carefully remove the poached egg with a slotted spoon and serve

Recipe 26

# How to Prepare a Mango

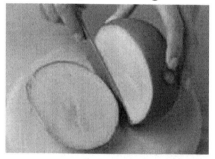

**Step 1.** Using a sharp knife, slice the mango lengthways on either side of the stone.

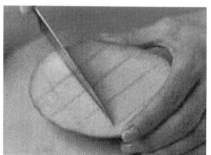

**Step 2,** Score a lattice into the flesh, being careful not to cut through the skin.

**Step 3** Gently push out the flesh, slice off the cubes and discard the skin. Cut the remaining flesh from around the stone into cubes and enjoy.

Recipe 27

## How to Prepare a Pineapple.

Our super sweet pineapples are grown in Costa Rica, where the climate produces intensely-flavoured fruit. They can be stored at room temperature for up to four days.

**Step 1**
Remove the leafy crown with a sharp knife and cut a thin slice from the base. Slice the skin away from top to bottom, removing any brown 'eyes' as you go.

**Step 2**

Carefully cut the pineapple in half lengthways and then into thick wedges.

**Step 3**

Remove the tough central core and discard.

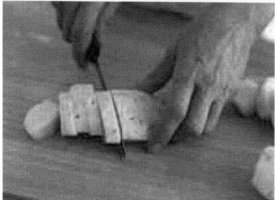

**Step 4**

Chop each wedge into bite-sized chunks

**Recipe 28**

## How to Prepare a Pomegranate

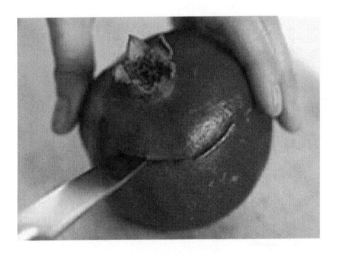

**Step 1**
Using a sharp knife, carefully slice about half an inch from the top of the pomegranate.

**Step 2**
Gently remove the lid to expose the edible seeds inside.

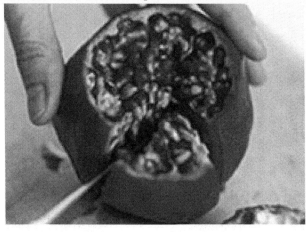

**Step 3**
Slice down through each of the white membranes inside the fruit.

**Step 4**
Pry the sections apart, turn the fruit inside out and pop the seeds out into a bowl.
**Tip**
Pomegranate juice stains, so it's a good idea to protect clothes and work surfaces.

Recipe 29

## How to Prepare a Whole Salmon

**Step 1**

Using scissors, cut away the gills, if still in place, to avoid the salmon tasting bitter.

## Step 2
Place in a fish kettle with white wine, herbs, whole peppercorns and lemon slices. Pour in cold vegetable stock or water, to halfway up the fish. Cover and bring slowly to the boil. Poach gently for 5-7 minutes.

## Step 3
Remove from the heat, and let the fish stand in the liquid for about 30 minutes if serving hot, or until cool. When cooked the dorsal fin should come away easily, if not, return to the boil, remove and cool again.

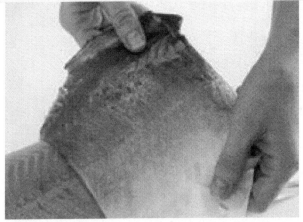

## Step 4
Run a sharp knife along either side of the fish, then carefully peel away the skin.

**Recipe 30**

## How to Prepare an Avocado

To avoid the flesh from discolouring, prepare avocados just before you serve them.

**Step 1**

Using a sharp knife, cut the avocado in half lengthways, carefully cutting around the fruit's large central stone.

**Step 2**
Twist the halves in opposite directions, until they come apart.

**Step 3**
Use a teaspoon to remove the stone.

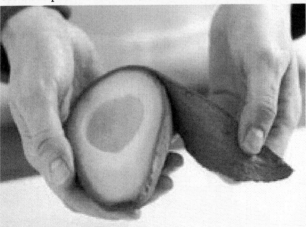

**Step 4**

Carefully peel the skin away from the flesh with your fingers or with the tip of a knife.

Recipe 31

## How to Prepare Leeks

Leeks need to be washed carefully, to remove any grit trapped in their layers.

**Step 1**

Trim off the roots and the coarse dark green part of the tops. Don't throw them away – they're great for adding to stocks.

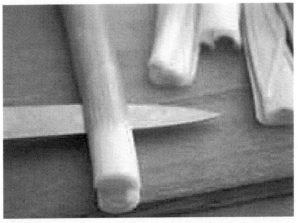

**Step 2**

Cut the leeks in half lengthways.

**Step 3**

Wash under a running tap, fanning the layers and rinsing away any grit or soil trapped between them.

**Step 4**

Drain thoroughly and slice as required.

**Recipe 32**

# How to Prepare Papaya

You can tell that a papaya is ripe from the slight orange blush on its yellowy green skin.

**Step 1**

Cut the papaya in half lengthways.

**Step 2**

Using a teaspoon, scoop out the black seeds and discard.

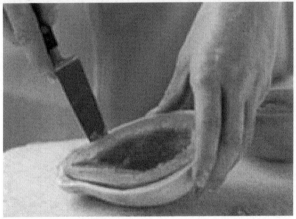

**Step 3**
Use a small sharp knife to cut the flesh away from the skin of each half.

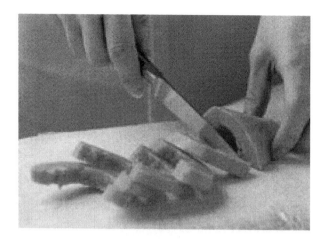

**Step 4**
Discard the skin and slice the flesh.

Recipe 33

# How to Shuck or to Open Oysters

Oysters are the ideal starter for a romantic Valentine's Day meal. Enjoy the fresh, briny taste as it is, or add extra kick with black pepper and fiery Tabasco sauce. Only use oysters that are shut or that close when tapped. Available from the fish service counter.

**Step 1** To shuck, or open, an oyster, grip it firmly in a clean tea towel and insert a knife into the hinged edge. Twist to open the shell.

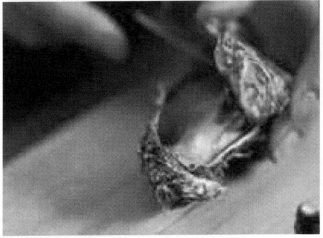

**Step 2** Run the knife along the inside of the top shell, cutting the muscle that attaches the oyster to the shell.

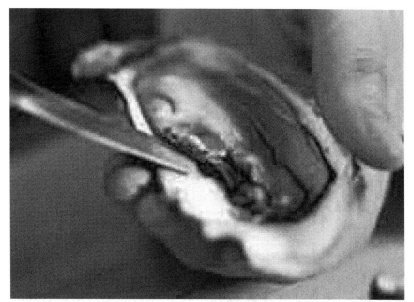

**Step 3** Lift off the top shell, then slide the knife under the oyster to cut the second muscle.

**Tip Oysters** will keep in the fridge for up to 24 hours.

Recipe 34

## How to Wilt Spinach

Fresh spinach needs only the very briefest cooking, to keep its colour and texture.

**Step 1**

If necessary, place spinach in a bowl of cold water, and leave for a few minutes until any grit drops to the bottom, or rinse under cold running water in a colander. Drain well.

**Step 2**

Heat a little olive oil in a large frying pan.

**Step 3**

Add the drained spinach, and allow to cook for about a minute, turning frequently.

**Step 4**

Add a knob of butter, season and sprinkle with freshly grated nutmeg. Toss together until the butter melts and serve immediately.

**Recipe 35**
# No-lump white sauce

**Serves: 8**

Prep 5 mins.   Cook 5 mins.

**Ingredients**

225ml milk

4 tablespoons olive oil

2 tablespoons plain flour

**Method**

In a small saucepan over medium heat, heat milk until warm. Do not boil.

In a separate bowl, mix the flour and oil together, then add a small spoonful of the warmed milk at a time, whisking until the mixture is runny and smooth.

Over medium heat, heat the entire mixture, whisking constantly. Turn off the heat at desired consistency. You can add anything to it, e.g., cheese, salt and pepper, parsley, garlic, chilli.

You can mix the oil and flour and leave in the fridge, using it as necessary for up to 3 months.

Recipe 36

## Cheesy white sauce

Serves 2.      Prep 5 mins.

Cook 8 mins.

## Ingredients

1 heaped tablespoon butter

1 heaped tablespoon plain flour

pinch of salt

250ml milk

225g grated cheese

## Method

Using a 700-watt microwave oven set at (adjust timing if using a higher wattage)

Melt the butter in a saucepan over a medium heat. Add the flour and salt and whisk until combined.

Add the milk. Whisk vigorously until there are no lumps.

Pour into a microwaveable safe jug or ceramic bowl, and microwave for 6 minutes, stopping every 2 minutes to whisk.

Add the cheese and microwave for a further 2 minutes. Whisk.

**Recipe 37**
# Four cheese sauce
**Serves 3.** Prep 10 mins.     Cook 10 mins.
## Ingredients

* 2 (227ml) pots double cream

- 100g butter
- 50g grated Parmesan cheese
- 50g grated mozzarella cheese
- 50g grated Provolone cheese
- 50g grated Pecorino cheese

**Method**

In a medium saucepan combine cream and butter. Bring to a simmer over medium heat, stirring frequently until butter melts. Gradually stir in cheeses. Reduce heat to low and continue to stir until all the cheese has melted.
Serve immediately, as the sauce will thicken upon standing.

**Tip:**
If you can't find Provolone which is a cheese from southern Italy, use any semi-hard cheese you prefer - Cheddar would do just fine.

**Parmesan cheese**
Parmesan cheese is not truly vegetarian, as it contains animal rennet. To make this dish 100% vegetarian, omit the cheese or find a suitable vegetarian substitute made without animal rennet. In supermarkets look for the 'parmesan style hard cheeses' which are suitable for vegetarians.

**Recipe 38**
## Onion béchamel sauce

**Serves: 4** Prep:15mins.  Cook 5 mins.

- **Ingredients**
- 600ml semi-skimmed milk
- 1 bay leaf
- 1 pinch grated nutmeg
- 6 black peppercorns
- 1 onion or 2 shallots, finely chopped
- 55g butter
- 55g plain flour

- salt and pepper
- **Method**
- Pour the milk into a heavy-based saucepan and add the bay 14 Prepper corns and nutmeg. Bring just to the boil over a moderate heat, then remove from the heat, cover and set aside to infuse for 10 minutes. Strain the flavoured milk into a jug.
- Melt the butter in the rinsed-out pan and cook and stir the onion or shallots for about 3 minutes until softened but not browned. Stir in the flour and cook gently, stirring occasionally, for 1 minute. Do not allow the flour to brown.
- Remove the pan from the heat and gradually pour in the milk, stirring or whisking constantly. Return the pan to the heat and bring to the boil, still stirring or whisking.
- Reduce the heat and simmer the sauce gently for 2 minutes, stirring occasionally, until it is smooth and thick. Taste and add salt and pepper.
- Serve or use immediately.

**Recipe 39**

## Spicy Tomato Sauce

**Serves: 4**

Prep 10 mins

Cook 15 mins.


1 Large onion, sliced

2 400g tins of chopped plum tomatoes

1 tsp ground cumin

1 tsp hot paprika

2 garlic cloves crushed salt and pepper to taste

Method

To make the sauce.

Add the sliced onion to the pan and cook on a low heat until it is very soft and just starting to brown. Add the tomatoes, garlic, ground cumin, hot paprika, crushed garlic cloves and the salt and pepper. Mix and leave to simmer for about 15 minutes. Keep watching it as you don't want it to get too thick. Now preheat the oven to 200C/ Gas Mark 6.

# Acknowledgements

### Give Credit Where Credit Is Due – aka Acknowledgments

"Miss" Bridget (Norfolk)

Margaret Van-Andel (Holland)

Ivan Self. Queensland (Australia)

Pam Howe. Sydney (Australia)

Sandra Earnshaw. (Devon)

Waitrose in their help in "How to"

Jacqui King (Lancashire)

Su Land (Lancashire)

Ina Wessels, Author, who is unfortunately no longer with us. (South Africa)

Barbara Thompson (The Borders)

## Disclaimer

We are not responsible for the outcome of any recipe you try from this book. You

may not achieve the results desired due to variations in ingredients, cooking

temperatures, typos, errors, omissions, or individual cooking ability. You should

always use your best judgement when cooking with raw ingredients such as eggs,

chicken or fish and seek expert advice before beginning if you are unsure. You

should always take care not to injure yourself or others on sharp knives or other

cooking implements or to burn yourself or others while cooking. You should

examine the contents of ingredients prior to preparation and consumption of these

recipes in order to be fully aware of and to accurately advise others of the presence of substances which might provoke an adverse reaction in some consumers. Recipes available in this book may not been formally tested by us or for us and we do not provide any assurances nor accept any responsibility or liability regarding their originality, efficacy, quality or safety.

Printed in Great Britain
by Amazon